D1425744

Cen

The Departure

<O K, everyone, let's get outta here,> Jake said wearily. He's always depressed after a battle.

Marco jokes after a battle. And before. But the jokes afterwards are always kind of strained.

Ax calmly wiped his tail blade off on the grass as we walked.

And I said, <I'm never doing that again.>

<Yeah, it was not a smart fight. But hey, we won,> Rachel said.

<No. I mean I am never doing that again,> I said. <*Never.* I quit. I quit this stupid war. I quit the Animorphs.>

I turned and walked away from the others. . .

Even the book morphs! Flip the pages and check it out!

Look for other ANIMORPHS titles
by K.A. Applegate:

ANIMORPHS

The Departure

K.A. Applegate

Hippo

For Michael and Jake

Scholastic Children's Books,
Commonwealth House, 1–19 New Oxford Street, London WC1A 1NU, UK
a division of Scholastic Ltd
London ~ New York ~ Toronto ~ Sydney ~ Auckland
Mexico City ~ New Delhi ~ Hong Kong

First published in the USA by Scholastic Inc., 1998
First published in the UK by Scholastic Ltd, 1999

Copyright © Katherine Applegate, 1998
ANIMORPHS is a trademark of Scholastic Inc.

ISBN 0 439 01142 6

All rights reserved

Printed by Cox & Wyman Ltd, Reading, Berks.

10 9 8 7 6 5 4 3 2

This book is sold subject to the condition that it shall not, by way of trade or
otherwise, be lent, resold, hired out, or otherwise circulated without the
publisher's prior consent in any form of binding or cover other than that in
which it is published and without a similar condition, including this
condition, being imposed upon the subsequent purchaser.

Chapter 1

My name is Cassie.

I am an Animorph. That's the name we made up for ourselves. Or actually, it's the name Marco made up for us. I'm not that clever with words.

I wish I was more clever with words. I really do. Because the story I have to tell is too strange, and in some ways too beautiful, for me to tell very well.

But I'll do the best I can. And later, when I can no longer tell the story, Jake will take over.

Here's what you need to know to begin with: we are not alone in the universe, we creatures of Earth. We humans are just one of maybe thousands of thinking, reasoning species. There are seven or eight that I know of for sure, ones that I have personally seen: Humans, Andalites, Yeerks, Hork-Bajir, Taxxons, Leerans, Gedds, Chee. And the Ellimists, if you can call them a species.

Among these species, the Yeerks move like a virus. They are parasites. Like intelligent tapeworms. They enter a body, wrap themselves around the brain and take over complete control.

Complete control. The poor creature who has been infested loses all power over his own actions. He loses all privacy. His memories are like a bunch of video-tapes that the Yeerk can play whenever he wants.

We call a human who has been taken over that way a Controller. The Hork-Bajir have all been made into Controllers. Well, almost all. The Taxxons, too. The Gedds.

And now the Yeerks are after the human race. They have invaded the body of the human race like a virus. Like a cancer. Unseen, unsuspected, growing, spreading, enslaving. . .

I guess you'd call them evil. I always did. An evil race. An evil species.

And I guess you'd say the Andalites are the opposite. The Andalites fight the Yeerks. It was a brave Andalite prince who broke his own laws to give us the power to morph. It's the only power we have to fight the Yeerks.

This is what I believed: that the Yeerks are evil. That the morphing power is all we have.

So I should have been glad to be able to fight the Yeerks. I should have been glad to have the morphing power.

I should have been glad. . .

<Cassie! Behind you!>

It was night. I was the wolf. I spun with far-more-than-human speed. I saw the Hork-Bajir's clawed, bladed foot slash towards me.

I jerked aside.

The foot landed in the dirt beside me, missing me by a hair. One centimetre to the left and it would have opened me up like a sardine can.

The Hork-Bajir was off-balance now. All his weight was on that foot. I could see the muscles rippling. I could see the tendons straining.

I lunged. I opened my jaw wide. I closed my teeth on those muscles, on those tendons, and I clamped with all the shocking power the wolf possessed.

I twisted my head savagely, ripping, tearing, trying to do damage.

"Rrrraaawwwr, raaawwrrr, rrrr!" I vocalized as I bit down. I repositioned, bit down again, and twisted and twisted, shaking my shoulders to help rip and tear.

The Hork-Bajir screamed in pain.

He tried to slash at me, but now he was off-balance in the other direction. He was falling back, thrown off by his own wild flailing.

3

He fell. The sound of his fall was sharp and clear and full of details to my incredible wolf hearing. My wolf sense of smell recorded the panic hormones, the Hork-Bajir equivalent of adrenaline that flooded his system.

My wolf ears could even hear the machine-gun pounding of his hearts. And the pulsing throb of the big arteries in his neck.

All around me, the battle raged. Jake, our unofficial leader, in tiger morph. Rachel as a huge, rampaging elephant. Marco, like me, a wolf. Tobias in his own hawk body, soaring and diving, attacking eyes and faces. And Ax, the Andalite, his sharp tail flailing like a bullwhip. A razor-tipped bullwhip.

We had been on a simple reconnaissance mission. It was a meeting of The Sharing, the front organization for Controllers. They were having a party for "new members". New members who thought they were joining something like the Boy or Girl Scouts, but would soon be dragged, willing or not, to be infested by Yeerks and be made slaves.

It was a barbecue in the park. A bonfire blazed. People ate hot dogs and coleslaw and slices of pie. The adults drank beer. The kids drank Cokes. The night sky was full of stars.

We had sneaked up close to the meeting in various morphs. We had identified a dozen people we did not know were Controllers. Including a

4

radio DJ who did one of those "wacky" morning shows, a policeman, a TV news reporter, and a supply teacher who I had for study time for two months while my regular study time teacher was having a baby.

A simple mission. Nothing too dangerous. Except that it had all gone wrong.

Far from the main meeting, off to one side, out of sight of the innocent, naive people who wanted to join "for the fun", the "executive meeting" had gone suddenly weird. One of the human-Controllers had made a mistake of some sort. A serious mistake. And suddenly, she was being hauled off towards a waiting Bug fighter by Hork-Bajir warriors.

They wanted to take her to Visser Three, the leader of the Yeerk invasion of Earth.

She knew what that meant. If she was lucky, her death would be quick. She started to yell.

"But I didn't do it! I didn't do it! You have to tell the Visser I'm innocent!"

That's when we changed our plans. That's when we decided to get involved. See, we figured if we saved the woman, the Yeerk in her head might co-operate with us. Might reveal secrets to us.

And we only saw two Hork-Bajir and a gaggle of human-Controllers, none of whom had a weapon.

So we'd morphed into battle morphs. And

that's when the other five Hork-Bajir had shown up.

We fought. Not exactly for the first time. And we were winning.

"Aaarrrggghhh!" the Hork-Bajir cried in panic and pain.

The Hork-Bajir's leg was in bad shape. I let go of it. I leaped up the length of his body. He slashed at me, but weakly. His night-sight was not as good as mine. He didn't see me as clearly as I saw him.

I saw his throat, unprotected.

<OK, they've had it, back away! Back away!> Jake yelled.

But it was too late for the Hork-Bajir. Too late to keep the wolf that was me from doing what its instincts taught it to do.

Too late.

We backed off. We stood for a moment, glowering at the battlefield. I could clearly hear the main group of The Sharing laughing and singing and having fun, off beyond this dark, bloody field. They were oblivious. They'd seen nothing.

But just beyond the battlefield stood a handful of human-Controllers. They stared at us with hatred.

We stared back at them.

And then we turned and melted away into the night.

<OK, everyone, let's get outta here,> Jake said wearily. He's always depressed after a battle.

<Seven of them, six of us, and we ruled!> Rachel said. She's usually up, almost giddy, after a battle.

Tobias was silent, as he usually is after a battle.

Marco looked for a joke. <You know, I was gnawing this Hork-Bajir's arm and I just kept thinking mustard. It would go so much better with mustard.>

Marco jokes after a battle. And before. But the jokes afterwards are always kind of strained.

Ax calmly wiped his tail blade off on the grass as we walked.

And I said, <I'm never doing that again.>

<Yeah, it was not a smart fight. But hey, we won,> Rachel said.

<No. I mean I am never doing that again,> I said. <*Never.* I quit. I quit this stupid war. I quit the Animorphs.>

I turned and walked away from the others.

I felt their eyes following me.

Maybe if I hadn't felt so hollow, so weak, so sickened inside, maybe I would have felt the extra set of eyes on me.

But I wasn't paying attention. I was done being afraid. I was done hurting other creatures.

I was done, done, *done* being an Animorph.

7

Chapter 2

I demorphed as I headed towards home. It started to rain a little, just a drizzle. Just enough to turn the leaves wet, to make the grass squishy as I walked across the field.

The lights were bright at my house. Through the family room window I could see my mum sitting at her desk going over paperwork.

I couldn't see my dad. But I knew where he was: in his big easy chair watching TV, the remote practically glued to his hand.

Our big barn was dark. Just a tiny, bright white light to mark the door so we could find it if one of the animals needed care in the night.

The barn is also the Wildlife Rehabilitation Clinic. Both my parents are vets. My mother works with the exotic animals at The Gardens, which is a zoo and amusement park. My dad runs the clinic, where he takes in injured wild animals: squirrels, geese, voles, foxes, deer, rabbits, bats, raccoons, hawks. You name it.

I help my dad in the barn. I give meds — medicines — to the animals. I clean them up and change bandages and feed them.

I headed for the barn to get the change of clothing I keep hidden there. See, when we morph, we can only morph the tight shirts and leotards we call our morphing outfits. I couldn't exactly show up back home wearing just that.

I didn't turn on the lights in the barn. I knew my way around. And I could see a red "Exit" light and light from the computer we used to keep track of the animals' progress.

I passed by the cages. Most of the animals were quiet. But not all were asleep. The nocturnal animals were pacing to and fro — those that could pace.

I walked by a fox. Its tail had been hacked off. Probably by some troubled kids. It paced and stared out of the cage and paced some more.

It looked at me. It had very intelligent eyes. It looked right at me.

"It's OK," I said to the fox.

I found my clothes in the tack room, changed, and walked to the house.

"Cassie! There you are." It was my dad. He

was kicked back in his easy chair, just like I knew he would be. "You didn't walk home, did you? It's raining."

"No, Rachel's mum gave me a ride."

"I didn't hear a car pull up."

I forced a laugh. "You were probably watching TV."

Lies came so easily. I had become an expert at lying since becoming an Animorph. But now there would be no need for lies.

"Yeah. This news story. A leopard's escaped from some fool who keeps exotic animals. They think it may have made it back up into the mountains. Clawed a man pretty badly. It'll be a tough job recapturing a leopard. Honey?" he yelled in a louder voice directed towards the kitchen. "Cassie's home."

My dad seemed way too perky. Way too cheerful. It was an act.

I went into bright light and gleaming linoleum. "Hi, Mum."

"Hi, sweetheart," my mum said.

Now my radar really tingled. My mother isn't one of those "honey-sweetheart" kind of people. Something was wrong. I felt my dad coming into the kitchen behind me.

"What's the matter?" I asked.

My parents sat down at the round table. I sat down, too. I was expecting a lecture about staying out too much. I was ready to promise not to do it again. I was ready to mean it, this time.

"There's no easy way to do this," my mum said. "Cassie, we've lost funding for the clinic. We just got word this evening."

I shot a look to my dad. He looked away and down and up at me, then away again.

"What do you mean?" I asked stupidly.

My dad muttered, "The, uh . . . the pet food company that's been paying to support the clinic is pulling out. I am trying to get a new company to help us out, but it doesn't look good. It looks like we're going to have to shut down the clinic."

I should have had something to say. They were both looking at me like I'd have something to say. But I just didn't.

"We know this will upset you," my mum said.

And I just stared blankly.

"We'll keep trying," my dad said. "In fact, I'm leaving town tomorrow to talk to a vice president at this new company."

I tried to find some words. But nothing. It was like every part of my life that mattered was being taken away in a single night. No more Animorphs. And I knew what that meant: Rachel would pretend to still be my friend, but she'd never really forgive me. Jake would still like me, but his life was about being leader of the Animorphs.

11

And now this. I was even losing my animals.

My mother was peering closely at me, looking bothered. "Um . . . honey, you have something in your teeth. Right there." She pointed to her own teeth.

I felt with my finger. I pulled out a small shred of something green and grey.

Somehow, while morphing from wolf back to human, it had become lodged between my shrinking teeth.

A small sliver of Hork-Bajir flesh.

Chapter 3

It took a long time for me to get to sleep.

I just kept thinking: it's all gone. Everything that was big and important in my life. All of it gone. My best friend. The guy I . . . that I liked. The animals I loved.

What was I going to do now? What was I going to *be*? I was just another short, slightly chubby girl now.

I had to tell Jake it was all a joke! I couldn't quit. Was I crazy? I couldn't quit!

But then, in the darkness, I saw that Hork-Bajir. I felt my powerful jaws grinding. . .

I've met a couple of free Hork-Bajir. The Hork-Bajir are a ferocious-looking race. Over two metres tall, with razor-sharp blades at their wrists, elbows, even on their legs and tail. But sometimes looks are deceiving. The Hork-Bajir use the blades to peel bark from trees back on their home planet. It's what they eat. They are peaceful herbivores.

It wasn't the fault of the Hork-Bajir. He hadn't done anything to me. It wasn't him trying to cut me up with his blades. It was the Yeerk in his head. That poor Hork-Bajir had no control of anything.

But he felt the pain. He suffered. He suffered because of what I did to him. And now, whatever hopes he might have had of someday being free, well, those hopes were gone.

Because of me.

"It was battle," I whispered into the sheets drawn up under my chin. "It's a war."

I hadn't heard Jake call us off. I hadn't heard in time. If I had, the Hork-Bajir might still have his dreams of freedom. And yet . . . when had Jake called us off? Before I lunged or after? It was all confused in my mind.

Confused. . .

I guess I drifted off to sleep, because I started to dream.

I was huge. Huge! More than thirteen metres long from my tail to my blunt, roaring head. Six metres tall. With teeth that were eighteen centimetres long.

I was the most dangerous predator the world has ever known.

I was Tyrannosaurus.

In the dark I saw the Triceratops slam its huge horns into another Tyrannosaurus. It was Marco, in morph just like me. He was on his side, his belly exposed to the horns.

I flexed the huge muscles in my tree trunk legs. I dug my massive bird-talons into the dirt. And I leaped!

Tonnes of muscle and bone soared through the air. I landed beside the Triceratops. I lowered my head, and opened my mouth and bit down into the exposed spine of the Triceratops. I sank my teeth into it and jerked back with all my might.

I felt the big dinosaur come up off the ground. Marco was safe. I knew that. But I was caught up now in the rage of battle.

I roared.

"HoooRRROOOOAAARRR!"

And the Triceratops screamed. "Rrrr-EEEE-EEEEEE! Rrrr-EEEEEEEEEE!"

I shook my Tyrannosaurus head, worrying the screaming Triceratops like a dog worrying a bone.

And then the Triceratops stopped making sounds. It hung limp. I dropped it and stood over the fallen creature. And I bellowed.

"Huh-huh-huh-RRRRRROOOOOAAAARRR!" I roared in triumph. The sound shook the leaves in the trees. It seemed to shake the distant stars.

"Huh-huh-huh-RRRRRROOOOOAAAARRR!" I screamed again.

I felt within me all the violence of nature, all

15

the ruthlessness of the survival of the fittest, all the power of muscle and bone and claw and tooth, all the ageless, never-ending lust for conquest wrapped into one awesome roar.

I woke up.

I jumped out of bed and ran to the bathroom in the hall. I closed the door and turned on the light. I sat there on the closed toilet for a while, shaking and holding my face with my hands.

I brushed my teeth.

I kept brushing my teeth till my gums were bleeding. With pink-stained toothpaste foaming around my mouth, I looked at myself in the mirror.

Was this what it was like to go nuts?

I opened the window. Cool night air flowed in. The rain had stopped. From here I could see the barn, quite close by. Soon it would be empty. No more animals.

I saw a flash of movement. Just a patch of darkness that shifted out of sight behind the barn. Probably an animal drawn to the smell and sounds of prey in the barn.

Only the eyes, the faint glimmer of eyes, did not come from low to the ground. It came from higher up. Like human eyes.

I stared for a while, and had the feeling that someone was staring back.

Then I closed the window and went back to bed.

Chapter 4

"**Y**ou weren't in school today," Jake said.

They had me surrounded. At least that's how it felt. We often met at the barn. It was one of our regular places. But it felt so different this time.

They were all there, all but Ax.

Jake stood, arms crossed over his chest. He was trying to look calm and relaxed. He wasn't succeeding. Something has happened to Jake during the months we've been Animorphs. He used to be just a normal kid. Good-looking, but not the kind girls got all giggly over. He had always looked solid and reliable and decent. The kind of guy to whom you wouldn't even suggest doing something wrong.

But even though there had always been

something "adult" about Jake, there was always still the kid underneath. That had changed. He had faced too many dangers. Worse, he had made too many life-and-death decisions.

That shows up in your face after a while. In your eyes. It showed up in the way Jake stood taller than before, and yet somehow a little worn-out. There was a ragged look to him.

"Yeah, I wasn't feeling well this morning," I said. "So I stayed at home."

"Maybe it was something you ate," Marco suggested with a smirk, laughing at his own wit.

Rachel snatched a towel off one of the cages and threw it at him. "That's not exactly helpful, Marco." She turned to me. "Look, everyone gets down about all this, OK? So take a couple of days to get your brain straightened out, take it easy, watch some telly, eat some cookies, and then you can come back."

Rachel had not been changed. Not that you could see. Rachel is one of these people who can walk through a hurricane, followed by a mud slide, followed by a flood, and come out clean, dry and with every hair in place.

She is still the tall, blonde, perfectly-accessorized girl she's always been. But inside, she, too, has changed. She'd always been bold. Now she was reckless. She'd always been aggressive. Now there were times when she scared me.

This war against the Yeerks had been a gift to Rachel. She'd found her true place in the universe. The world would probably never have allowed pretty Rachel to become the warrior she was meant to be. But being an Animorph, she'd become all that.

"Look," I said, "I know what you all think. You think I'm just upset because of one battle last night. But that's not it."

I opened a cage containing a goose whose wing had been mauled by a wildcat. I began to cut away the old bandage.

<So if it wasn't the battle last night, what was it?> Tobias asked.

Of us all, Tobias has suffered the most. He is a red-tailed hawk. At first he was trapped in that form, unable to escape, unable to morph at all. But then the Ellimist gave him back his power to morph. Even to morph into his old human body.

There was just one catch. If Tobias stays in morph again — any morph, even his own human body — he will be trapped again. And this time the Ellimist will not save him.

Tobias could become human again. But if he did, he would lose the ability to morph. He would be out of the fight against the Yeerks.

I don't know why Tobias has chosen to remain a hawk. I guess he wants to stay in the war. Or maybe the truth is, he's happier as a hawk than he was as a human.

I looked at him, sitting with his talons gripping a wooden cross beam high up towards the slanted roof of the barn. "I guess I'm not you, Tobias. I guess I'm not willing to make the sacrifices you've made."

"What sacrifices?" Rachel demanded, getting angry now. "We have the chance to save the planet! How can you talk about sacrifices? There are thousands, maybe millions, of people still enslaved by the Yeerks. Who's going to save them if not us?"

"I don't know," I said. I finished removing the goose's bandage and began cleaning the wounds.

"This is bogus," Marco said bitterly. "You know, back when we started all this, it was me who didn't want to get involved. And you all acted like I was a big coward, or else selfish."

I shrugged. "So I'm a coward. I'm selfish."

Marco practically leaped at me. His eyes were blazing. "What's the deal with you, Cassie? Half the time you're giving us all crap over being too ruthless or whatever. It's always, 'Oh, is this *right*?' and 'Oh, *should* we do this?' I mean, you're Miss Morality, and then when you have a bad night you just bail out on us?"

"That's not what it's about," I said. I could feel something like pressure on my heart. Like something was pushing to get out of me. Something explosive.

"Oh? So what then? You just want to spend more time playing with your animals?"

"The Wildlife Rehabilitation Clinic is going to be shut down," I said. "No money."

I guess that just puzzled Marco. He fell silent.

"So no, I guess I won't be spending my time playing with the animals," I said sarcastically.

"Cassie, we need to understand this," Jake said wearily. "We need to understand you."

"She's scared," Marco sneered.

"Marco, shut up," Rachel snapped. "She's not scared."

"Yes, I am," I said.

"You are not," Rachel said, waving her hand like I was some annoying fly. "You're as brave as any of us. Just because you have all these moral qualms and feel bad over stuff, that doesn't make you a coward."

"I destroyed that Hork-Bajir," I said.

Rachel's blue eyes went cold and seemed to look past me. "It's a war. They started it. Of course you feel bad over—"

"No," I said. "I didn't feel bad. I heard Jake say to back off. And after he said that, *after* he said that, I did it."

I wasn't sure that was true. But I needed to say it. To make them understand.

No one had anything to say for a while. I started putting the new bandage on the goose.

"So you feel bad about it," Rachel said with a shrug.

"No. I feel bad because I felt nothing. I felt . . . nothing, Rachel. At that moment I felt like I was just doing my job, you know? And now they're shutting down the clinic, and my dad tells me and I feel . . . nothing. It's been going on for a long time. Each day, each battle, each mission, I just *feel* less and less."

I looked at Rachel. She looked away. I turned to Jake. He made the ghost of a smile and nodded his head. He understood. He knew. It was happening to him, too. But then he looked away as well.

I spread my hands, open, helpless. "I can't *not* feel anything when there's violence. I can't *not* care about living things. I can't be like that."

Marco laughed a short, brutal laugh. "Fine. You have your morals and your fine feelings and all that. We'll go off and risk our lives to save the world. You just sit here and feel righteous."

He left. I heard the flutter of wings and realized Tobias had gone, too.

Rachel had an expression I've almost never seen on her face: she was hurt.

"Rachel, we can still be—"

"No, we can't," she said, cutting me off. "See, you've just said the whole world can drop dead, so long as *you*, Cassie, don't have to end up turning into *me*." She stormed from the barn.

I should have said something. But it was true. It was true I didn't want to turn into Rachel.

Jake and I were alone. He looked down at the ground. "Don't morph," he said. "If you're not an Animorph, don't use the power."

"I won't."

"You'll want to," he said. "But if you do, you run the risk of getting caught. Those risks are acceptable if you're going to help us. But if you're not in the fight any more, you can't use the weapon."

"I said I wouldn't morph any more, Jake. I'm not a liar."

He left. I stood there, all alone with the animals. The goose was still half-bandaged. Animals needed their meds. Some needed feeding.

And I didn't care.

Chapter 5

I had fallen behind on a lot of my chores. One was the water trough made from an old claw-foot bathtub that we kept in a far corner of the pasture for the horses. It had got overgrown with algae and was crusted with windswept leaves.

I rode one of the horses out there. Riding a horse has always made me feel better, and besides, I'd got slack about exercising the horses. I took my favourite mare.

It was a cool, gusty afternoon with clouds rolling in again, threatening an early sunset. I rode at a trot most of the way, feeling chilly air on my face and trying to think of nothing.

But when I got to the old tub, I found it perfectly clean. No leaves, no algae. It had even been propped up to sit more level on the ground.

I swung down out of the saddle and looked around for an explanation. I found it in the mud: a narrow hoofprint, not much different from a deer's. You'd think it was a deer print if you didn't know to look very carefully.

It was an Andalite hoofprint. Obviously Ax had seen that the trough needed work and had taken care of it.

This part of the pasture was right up against the forest. The grass stopped just a couple of metres past the fence, and there the line of trees began. I looped the mare's reins over the fence and looked around.

Grassland sweeping back towards my house, which was invisible from this angle. And trees which I knew swept all the way back to the distant mountains.

I hadn't thought about not morphing any more. I hadn't realized I'd be giving that up. The ability to become a bird and fly. The ability to become all the animals I had loved for so long. To see the world through their eyes and hear with their ears.

I sighed. Jake was right, of course. I couldn't run the risk. Not now. Not if I wasn't going to contribute.

"Who cares?" I asked the breeze.

But as much as I didn't want to care, I did. About this one thing, I cared. Life just seemed so cramped and small without being able to morph ever again.

Then I saw it. Just a movement behind the front row of trees. I didn't see what had moved, just that there was a movement.

Was it Ax?

"Nee-EEEE-he-he-he!" The horse whinnied. She tossed her head.

My mind flashed to the escaped leopard. Could he have made it this far? No. Not likely.

Besides, what I'd seen moving in the trees wasn't a leopard. You didn't see leopards unless they wanted to be seen. And whatever I'd seen, or almost seen, had not moved with the liquid grace of a leopard.

"Ax!" I yelled.

No answer.

I mounted the mare again and tried to ease her into a trot. But she reared up and neighed loudly.

Something was bothering her. But what? And where was it? I licked my finger and held it up to feel the breeze. It was blowing from the direction of the trees.

"Easy, now. Easy," I said.

The wind shifted direction. The mare calmed. This just worried me more. It confirmed that she had smelled something in the woods. Now that the wind was coming from a different direction, she no longer smelled what had been bothering her.

Then—

CRASH! CRASH! CRASH!

"Aaaaahhhhh!"

A flash of red hair, running.

And behind it, a much bigger creature, running like a bowling ball, almost seeming to roll.

A bear!

A black bear was chasing a girl with red hair.

The girl ran, but the bear was far too fast. The girl leaped towards a low branch, snagged it and scrambled wildly up into the tree.

But it wouldn't help. If the bear wanted her, it would climb right up the tree after her!

Before I knew what I was doing, I tightened my grip on the reins and urged the mare forward.

"Giddap! Hah! Hah!"

We ran along the fence, hooves pounding. I could see the girl dangling, barely holding on. And then I saw what I had feared: behind the black bear was a cub. Bears are seldom aggressive towards humans. Unless the human makes the big mistake of somehow getting too close to a cub.

The black bear was ripping at the slender tree. The girl screamed in terror.

I yanked the mare away from the fence, backed off thirty metres, then said, "Hee-yah!" and dug my heels in, urging her to run towards the fence.

We galloped, tearing up clods of damp dirt and grass behind us. I tucked down, held on tight and hoped the mare knew how to jump, because I sure didn't.

Up! Up! We sailed high—
WHAP!

Her back hooves caught the top rail and then landed hard but safe. "Come on, girl!" I yelled, and we raced towards the tree.

The horse was terrified, eyes wide, mouth foaming. But she was in a panic run now, and horses never have been the geniuses of the animal world. So she ran straight for the bear.

The girl was hanging from a branch by her fingertips.

"Hang on, I'll get you!" I screamed.

Ten metres more . . . seven metres . . . three metres. . .

The girl screamed.

She dropped.

The bear roared.

I grabbed at the air. One hand found the front of a Levi's jacket. I held on, yanked her towards me, and sped on.

Twigs whipped my face. One foot was out of its stirrup and I was gasping for breath.

I scrabbled desperately, trying to find the stirrup without being able to look down. The girl was strangling me, holding on for dear life. I dropped the reins. The mare was in a blind panic.

And with good reason. Because the bear wasn't done with us.

The bear was chasing us.

In open country we'd outrun the bear easily. But in the brush, the bear was keeping up.

Then, quite suddenly, the bear gave up the chase and calmly walked back to her cub. The mare, however, was not ready to stop running. And I could not reach the reins. All I could do was hold on. Hold on to a handful of mane and the girl's jacket.

Suddenly—

No more trees ahead of us. The river! White water, swollen by the recent rains, bounding and crashing over rocks.

The mare was pelting towards it. I tried once more to reach the reins. I slipped. I grabbed a handful of mane and yanked myself back up.

And in a split second I saw the low branch. WHAM!

I felt myself flying, flying, flying. . .

But by the time I hit the water, I wasn't feeling anything at all.

Chapter 6

"**A**aaahhhh!"

I woke up screaming.

I was in a boiling, mad, lunatic current. Water rushed around me, over me. Water filled the air. It twisted me over and over like a corkscrew.

I flailed my arms, but they barely moved. I couldn't feel my hands or fingers. My legs felt dead. I was freezing. Freezing to death.

THUMP!

I hit a rock and barely felt the impact on my side.

Then . . . falling, falling! I saw trees that seemed to fly up and away from me. I saw a glimpse of explosive white water beneath me. I was falling, the water vertical around me.

PAH-LOOSH!

I was all the way underwater, and being pounded viciously by the waterfall. It sounded like some monstrous engine, throbbing, beating, hammering at me.

FWOOSH! FWOOSH! FWOOSH! FWOOSH! FWOOSH!

I tried to swim, but my arms were made of jelly. My fingers were stiff as sticks. *Morph!* I told myself. But I couldn't concentrate. Couldn't hold the thought in my brain.

Suddenly, I shot clear of the beating waterfall, but I was still underwater. Far underwater. Too far.

I tried to hold my breath, but I was becoming more and more confused. What . . . where . . . which way should I . . . arms. . .

I sucked air into my burning lungs.

Only it wasn't air.

I gagged and writhed, helpless. Suffocating! My head bumped on something. A rock? The surface! I could see it. Now it was just centimetres over my head.

Just centimetres of water separated me from the air.

But it was too late. I closed my eyes. My muscles relaxed. I went to sleep.

I didn't feel the arms that hauled me up out of the water. I didn't feel the mouth that breathed air into me.

31

"Hah! Wah?" I woke up! Then instantly felt my insides heave.

"Buh-buh-leaaahhh!"

I threw up. I was on my back in the dirt. I vomited all over myself.

I rolled my head to one side and sucked in air, coughed, breathed, coughed some more. I hacked away for several minutes, gasping for a good clean breath with lungs still wet from the river.

A sharp pain in my side. A splitting headache. Pins and needles in my frozen hands and feet so intense it made me want to scream.

But I was alive!

Only then did I notice the girl. She was squatting just a metre or so away. Her red hair was wet and bedraggled, plastered against her forehead and hanging in long, soggy curls.

She had brilliant green eyes that seemed unnaturally large. She was wearing jeans, a T-shirt, and a denim jacket. She was shivering.

"You saved my life, didn't you?" I said to her in a hoarse, raspy voice.

"You saved mine," she said. "That bear could have killed me. So now we're even. I don't owe you anything and you don't owe me."

It was a strange thing to say. Too mature . . . I don't know, too *old* to be coming from someone so young.

I sat up, fighting the urge to cry from the

pins and needles feeling. "My name is Cassie."

"I'm Karen."

"Where are we?"

She shook her head. "I don't know. We were in the river for a long time. I was knocked out, too. But I came to sooner than you. And I was able to grab on to a floating log for part of the time."

I looked around. The trees were very tall, mostly pines. I saw no obvious trails. No rubbish or other signs of humans. We were deep in the forest.

I tried to form a mental picture of the course of the river. I knew it came down from the mountains, fed by melting snow and rain. It swept very near our farm, then doubled back, heading towards the mountains until the slope changed again and turned it at last towards the sea.

But that didn't tell me where we were. We could be a kilometre from civilization, or we could be ten kilometres. But more troubling was that I didn't know what direction to go. If we went the right way, we might hit a road pretty soon. If we went the wrong way . . . well, the forest was very large. You could be lost in the forest for a long, long time.

"Did you ever read *Hatchet* by Gary Paulsen?" I asked Karen.

"No."

"I did. I wish I'd paid more attention. I'm not exactly an expert on wilderness survival tactics. Besides, we don't seem to have a hatchet. Guess we'll just have to take our best guess and walk out of here."

Karen looked solemnly at me. "My ankle is hurt. I can't walk."

I took a deep breath. I was mostly revived now. I could feel my hands and feet again. And my brain was starting to work a little better, too.

"Karen, what were you doing there in the woods to begin with?"

She didn't answer. She just looked at me.

I felt a new kind of chill. "The other night, someone was behind the barn, looking up at my window. That was you, wasn't it?"

She said nothing.

I felt an awful dread begin to well up inside me. I felt like I couldn't breathe.

"Why were you following me? Why were you spying on me?" I demanded, trying not to panic, but already feeling the terror growing inside me, churning my stomach, squeezing my heart.

Karen sighed. Then she cocked her head and looked at me quizzically. Like I was some interesting specimen of insect and she was an entomologist.

"You interest me," she said.

"There's nothing interesting about me. Really."

"Sure there is. See, if I'm right about you, then you can fly away from this place any time you want. If I'm right about you, you can also . . . let's just say, make a few changes . . . and kill me."

I forced an awful fake laugh. "What on earth are you talking about?"

"Oh, nothing on *Earth*," Karen said. "At least that's what everyone believes. Humans can't morph. Only Andalites can morph. Only an Andalite could become a wolf and rip the throat from my brother's host body and leave him dying."

Chapter 7

I guess Marco would have been cooler, more glib. Maybe Rachel would have just attacked. I don't know. But I'm not Marco or Rachel.

I stared, breathing stopped.

"I have no idea what you're talking about," I said.

Karen smiled a small, triumphant smile. "I followed you after that battle. You separated from the others and went your own way to that farm. I saw you loping along as a wolf one minute, then I lost sight for a few minutes. But when I caught up again, there was no wolf. Just you. Seemingly a human girl."

"What do you think I am? A werewolf or something?" I asked, trying out my desperate, fake laugh again.

"I don't know what you are," Karen said. "Not for sure. That's why I followed you. See, everyone knows there's a band of Andalite warriors here on Earth. It makes sense that they would try to pass as humans. But everyone also knows no Andalite can stay in a morph more than two hours. And I've seen you in this human morph for more than two hours at a time."

I shrugged and put on a baffled expression. "OK, whatever. Maybe the cold water messed up your brain a little or something. Maybe we should just focus on getting you some help."

"I know you're not an Andalite who's been trapped in a morph because you morphed that wolf the other night. So that leaves two possibilities. Either you are an Andalite who has somehow figured out how to defy the two-hour limit. Or. . ."

"Or what?" I couldn't help asking.

"Or what some of us have suspected for some time is true: there are humans who can morph."

I shrugged. "Are you like one of those *X-Files* people?" I asked.

Karen smiled. "If you're an Andalite, you'll just demorph and kill me. This little human body would be defenceless against your tail."

"Now I have a tail?"

"If you're a human who can morph, then you'll morph something nasty and kill me that way."

"So, wait a minute. Let me get all this

37

straight. In this little fairy tale of yours, I'm capable of destroying you either way, right?"

She cocked her head in a very human gesture. "You'll *think* you can," she said. "And whatever you do, I'll have proof."

I stood up. I'm not exactly tall enough to tower over anyone or look very threatening. But still, Karen should have looked just a little bit nervous. Instead she looked smug. Cocky. Like she was just waiting to see what I'd do.

I stuck out my hand. "Come on, crazy girl," I said, "let's get started. It may be a long walk back."

There was a flicker of doubt in those cool, green eyes. She ignored my hand and tried to stand. Half-way up, her left leg buckled and she fell back heavily.

"My ankle is badly injured," she said. "I'm afraid I can't walk."

I looked down at her and ran through my options.

In this forest there were bears and wolves. The bears wouldn't attack her as long as she stayed out of their way. But the wolves might, if they were hungry enough. The woods around us looked empty, silent. But I have been a wolf. I know the awesome power of their senses. I was willing to bet that at least one wolf pack already knew we were there. They'd heard us, they'd smelled us.

If they were hungry enough, they'd come by to check out the unfamiliar smell. If they came and saw a helpless kid, unable to walk, defenceless . . . well, wolves aren't man-eaters by nature, but they are programmed to take down the weak and sick.

And if the wolves didn't get her, there was the cold night and the hunger. If I walked away now, the human-Controller named Karen could very possibly not survive the night. Killed by nature's hand.

One thing was certain. If Karen made it back to her fellow Controllers, knowing what she knew, none of my friends were safe. She knew I was an Animorph. Or had been one. It would be easy for her to find out who my friends were. To take them, one by one, and make them submit to infestation. Make them into Controllers.

All it would take was one: me, Jake, Rachel, Marco. It didn't matter. If the Yeerks controlled one of us, all our secrets would be theirs.

They would learn of the hidden colony of free Hork-Bajir up in the mountains. They would learn about the Chee — the peace-loving androids who sometimes helped us with information.

If Karen came out of this alive, Jake, Rachel, Marco, Tobias and Ax would all be caught and made into human-Controllers or be killed. The Chee would be annihilated. The Hork-Bajir would be recaptured.

All hope for human freedom might die. Unless . . . unless Karen was destroyed right here, right now.

I turned away and walked to a dried-out, fallen tree. I grabbed a long, forked branch. I levered my weight against it and worked it until it splintered and cracked.

It was a strong, stout branch. One metre long, thick, with a fork at one end. I gripped it tightly and carried it back to Karen. One swift, sure blow to the head. That's all it would take. I could knock her out and leave her tied up with her own shoelaces and let nature do the rest.

I saw the apprehension in her eyes.

"Here," I said. "This will make a good crutch. Wait here while I find some smaller sticks to make a splint."

Chapter 8

We were not in a good position. Night was falling. We were somewhere in a forest. We had no tools and no matches. Everything around us was damp, maybe too damp to burn. And what I could see of the sky, looking up through the trees, was filled with dark clouds scudding on a stiff breeze.

"This will hurt," I said. I had found some sticks the right length. I had removed my belt. Fortunately, I never listen to Rachel on matters of fashion, so I had a good, strong, practical leather belt.

"Your trousers will fall down," Karen said, sounding like a kid again.

"Yeah, right. I seem to have gained a little weight since I bought these trousers. They're plenty tight. Or maybe they shrank. That could be it." I placed the sticks carefully around her lower leg and down over her ankle bone. Then I wrapped the belt loosely. "OK, I'm not going to tighten it a lot, because your ankle is going to swell up. But I have to tighten it some. I want to keep your ankle immobilized. On the count of five, OK? When I get to five, I'll yank it. One. . ."

I yanked the belt.

"Aaahhh! Hey! What happened to five?"

"You would have tensed up on five," I said. "This way I caught you while you were relaxed."

"A trick."

"For your own good."

Karen snorted. "Now I know you're an Andalite. Typical Andalite arrogance. The only race in the entire galaxy that makes war 'to help people'."

I stood up again and stuck out my hand. This time, Karen took it. "Come on," I said. "We have to get moving."

I helped her to her feet. She winced in pain as she placed weight on the bad ankle. I leaned over awkwardly to grab the crutch. "Here. Try this."

She stuck it under one arm. "Which side? The side with the bad ankle, or the other side?"

"I don't know," I admitted. "I don't work with humans much."

"Ah? Ready to stop pretending and admit what you are, Andalite?"

I laughed. A real laugh this time. "I work with animals. I know how to set a broken leg on a deer or a raccoon or a wolf. I've never done a human before."

Karen peered sceptically. "Ah, yes. The barn full of animals. Of course. What a perfect cover for an Andalite. All those animals right there so you can acquire their DNA for morphing."

"Whatever you say, kid," I muttered. "Let's try moving."

"Where are we going? Which way is civilization?"

"I don't have a clue. But it doesn't matter. We're not trying for a way out, not tonight, anyway. We need shelter."

"What? If you're going to try to kill me, go ahead and do it. No need to drag me off to some secluded spot."

"Karen, what could possibly be more secluded than this?" I waved my arm around at the tall trees.

"OK, if you don't have the stomach for killing me, let's walk out of here. My leg is fine." She took a couple of wincing steps.

"Look, I'm sorry you think I'm some space alien. I'm sorry you think I want to kill you. But the truth is, if we try and walk out of here tonight, we could end up dead. It's going to rain. Maybe even storm. You ever been in a forest in the middle of a storm? The ground will be mud.

Lightning hitting the trees. Flash floods in the gullies. Cold. No way to build a fire. You wouldn't like it."

Suddenly Karen erupted in a rage. "Why do you keep up this stupid game? I know what you are capable of! I know what you did. You could morph to that wolf and easily kill me and then run out of these woods. Why are you playing this game?!"

I waited till she was done yelling. Then I said, "I see higher ground over that way. Maybe low hills. I can't tell, peering through these trees. Maybe we'll find a cave over there. At least we'll be away from this river. It could rise during the night, with rain and all."

But Karen wasn't listening any more. She was staring up at a tree.

"What is that?" she asked in a worried voice.

I followed the direction of her gaze. There, lodged in a crook of an elm tree branch, was a crumpled, ripped body. The sweet face with the big eyes was lolled to the side.

"It's a young deer," I said.

"What's it doing up there?"

"The animal that killed it put it there for safe-keeping."

"What kind of animal does that? A wolf? A bear?"

I shook my head. "No. But a leopard does."

Chapter 9

I read a book by this hunter once. He had hunted lions. He'd hunted tigers. He'd hunted bears. But he said of all the dangerous animals a man could hunt, nothing was as dangerous as a leopard.

They were smart, adaptable, cunning and ruthless. They were the ultimate hunters.

Human hunters, professional, experienced hunters armed with high-powered rifles and telescopic sights, had waited in trees for hours for a leopard to return to the place where it had stashed a kill. They had waited with eyes wide-open, nerves tingling, guns at the ready . . . and had suddenly felt the faint tingling warning that they were being watched. And they had turned to find the leopard sitting right behind them in the tree. The last thing they ever saw.

"A leopard? Are you kidding? This isn't Africa."

"One escaped from a sort of private zoo," I said.

"From a private zoo? So it's probably tame, right?"

"It put a man in the hospital," I said.

All the while I swept my eyes back and forth through the trees. It could be watching us. It could be watching us right now. It could have our scent in its nostrils.

I took a deep breath. Then another. I *saw* nothing. Which *proved* nothing. I wouldn't see the leopard unless it wanted to be seen.

"Maybe we'd better build a fire," Karen said. "Wild animals are scared of fire."

"Yeah. Let's get to some shelter, then build a fire," I agreed. There was no need to tell Karen that she was wrong: fire doesn't frighten most predators. Certainly not leopards. In African villages, leopards come right into the village, right into the huts, right past the fires, and drag dogs and pigs . . . and children . . . away.

"Let's get moving," I said tersely.

I started walking, slowly, waiting to see how well Karen could keep up. She couldn't. Not very well. She took a dozen steps and caught her crutch on a root and fell down. I helped her up. On the second try she went further before becoming entangled in a bush.

All the while the shadows deepened around us. Already we could see no more than thirty metres through the trees. We had to move faster. I put my arm around Karen's shoulders.

"Keep your filthy hands off me, Andalite!" she spat.

I didn't remove my arm. "You know, I don't know who these Andalites of yours are, Karen, but you sure seem to have a grudge against them."

She laughed. "We don't exactly get along with Andalites."

"Who is 'we'?" I asked, to make it seem like I didn't already know.

We started walking again. Karen was beginning to get the hang of the crutch. I kept looking up at the trees. Leopards often kill by dropping from a tree on to an unwary prey.

"Who is 'we'?" Karen echoed. "We are the Yeerks. The Yeerk Empire."

"I see. So you Yeerks and these Andalites don't like each other." The ground sloped upwards. It was a gentle enough slope, unless you were trying to walk with a bad ankle and a tree branch for a crutch.

"The Andalites are the busybodies of the galaxy," Karen said. "Always sticking their noses in other people's business. We have a right to expand. We have a right to advance. But you Andalites don't see it that way, do you? No,

47

the whole galaxy has to belong to the mighty Andalites."

She was trying to provoke me. She was trying to get me to make some answer that would give away the fact that I was not a normal human girl.

"So if I'm an Andalite, and these Andalites are such rotten people, why am I helping you?" I asked.

Karen considered for a while. "I don't know," she admitted.

"Well, maybe you're just totally wrong about me, have you considered that? Maybe I'm not a werewolf or an Andalite or anything but a normal girl."

She said nothing to that. We walked on through darkening gloom. I began to pick up small twigs and sticks that looked fairly dry.

We reached the base of a sort of low ridge that cut straight across our path. It was no more than fifteen metres high for the most part. We turned right to follow along the ridge because going left was rougher terrain.

Vast rocks jutted up out of the earth. Fallen leaves covered the slope. Scraggly trees clung to the slope and larger trees lined the ridge itself.

Then, all at once, it was raining. The rainfall clattered noisily down through the leaves of the trees. Within minutes I was as wet as I'd been when I came from the river.

"In there." I pointed.

"I don't see anything."

"Behind those bushes, that shadow. That may be a cave."

It would mean forcing my way through a thicket of brambles. Karen wouldn't even be able to attempt it until I'd made a path. And the cave might not even be there.

Or worse. There might be a cave that was already taken by a bear or even a mother wolf, raising a family.

"Use your tail," Karen said. "You'll cut right through."

I sighed noisily. "How about if I just push my way through? I'll need your crutch to knock some of the bushes down. Why don't you sit on that rock?"

Karen sat on the rock. I took the crutch and began beating away at the bushes. I deliberately made as much noise as possible. If something was living in the cave, I wanted it to be warned. You don't want to surprise bears. You just don't.

As I got closer, it became clear that there really was a cave. I looked around in the dirt to see if I could spot any tracks. But with the rain, who could tell?

I glanced back. I could barely see Karen. She certainly could not see me. The smart thing to do was to morph now. Maybe the wolf again. The wolf's nose would instantly know whether

49

there was anything in the cave.

I crouched low. I focused my mind on the wolf DNA that was a part of me. And, with a Controller no more than seven metres away, I began to morph.

Chapter 10

I felt my legs dwindle in size, but not weaken. I felt my chest and shoulders swell and become large. My face began to bulge outwards.

If you're not an Animorph, don't use the power.

I heard Jake's voice in my head. It startled me, it was so clear in my memory.

I won't. That's what I'd said.

You'll want to. But if you do, you run the risk of getting caught. Those risks are acceptable if you're going to help us. But if you're not in the fight any more, you can't use the weapon.

I said I wouldn't morph any more, Jake. I'm not a liar.

I stopped morphing. I was still half-human. But I was also half-wolf. And already my hearing was more acute than any human hearing.

I heard the sound of the bushes being parted. I heard the sound of a dragged foot and a slight gasp of pain.

Karen! She was trying to spy on me.

I demorphed as quickly as I could. At the same time, I pushed ahead, shoving my way through the bushes with the crutch. No choice now. I couldn't morph. I'd promised Jake I wouldn't. Besides, I'd almost got caught.

I found a roughly triangular gap in some tumbled stones. Definitely a cave. Once more I searched the ground. No tracks. I tried to see if any fur had been caught by the brambles, but now the rain was pouring in a torrent.

I crept close to the cave opening. And I sniffed the air. The human sense of smell is pathetic compared to that of a dog or a wolf. Still, maybe I would be able to tell if something was living in the cave.

Closer . . . closer, I crept. . .

"Aaahhhh!"

I jumped back. I fell. Had I screamed? No, I was confused. It was Karen's voice.

"Ahh! Ahhh! Help me!"

A trick!

Maybe. Maybe not. I ploughed back through the brush. I emerged, panting, scratched and muddy, in time to see the leopard leap from the tall rock down towards the helpless girl.

TSEEEWWW!

A Dracon beam sliced upwards at the leopard.

"Rrrraaww-rrrr!" the leopard screamed. But the Dracon beam had only grazed the big cat's shoulder. It hit the ground, rolled easily to its feet, and turned to attack again.

Karen tried to steady the Dracon beam for a shot. But her bad ankle twisted and collapsed. She fell face-forward. The Dracon beam clattered over some rocks and landed in the mud.

It landed within centimetres of the leopard.

Everything was frozen. Karen, aghast that she'd dropped her weapon. Terrified.

The leopard, unsure, watching, waiting, trying to assess.

And me. Did I have time to morph? Would it just set the leopard off? Would it make him want to attack?

"Karen," I said in a low voice. "Crawl towards me."

"That thing . . . that thing will. . ."

"Karen, listen to me. Crawl towards me."

She was trembling. Barely able to pick her face up out of the mud. She kept her eyes glued to the leopard. Her green eyes seemed huge, shining out of the mud that covered her face.

The leopard watched her with the intensity of a predator. Then it looked at me. It was unsure. Worried. It was seeing things it had never seen before.

You could almost watch the cunning mind working behind those cold, yellow eyes: the smaller prey had used a weapon. But that weapon had gone now. Still, the hunter had to be cautious when the hunted could sting.

And then, the leopard thought, there was this curious, second creature. The one whose scent was changing.

<Karen,> I said. <Keep crawling this way. Don't rush. Don't stop, but don't jerk or rush in any way.>

I don't know if Karen even noticed that she was no longer hearing my voice. She kept her gaze riveted on the leopard.

"Ooof!" Her arm slipped and she rolled over in the mud.

The leopard saw her bare white throat and made its decision.

He leaped!

I leaped! I landed first. I bristled, snarled, and raised the thick grey fur around my neck.

The leopard saw my teeth and forgot about Karen's throat.

No, no, the leopard thought, *I don't need a fight with another predator. There will be plenty of time to kill the little, helpless one later.*

The leopard turned, and with infinite contempt, walked away into the darkness.

And Karen picked her face up out of the mud and looked at me.

"So," she said shakily. "I guess you are a werewolf, after all."

Chapter 11

The cave was unoccupied. I found that out very quickly, using the wolf's senses.

It took much longer to build a fire. I'd done it once before. Built a fire without matches, that is. It was in the Cretaceous Period, during a very bizarre episode in our lives as Animorphs.

It had been hard to do then. It was harder to do now. The wood was wet and the grass I used for kindling was damp as well, although it dried out faster than the wood did.

We had to keep the fire near the entrance of the cave, since it was very smoky at first. But eventually we got it going.

We sat there, cross-legged, on hard stone and cold sand. We huddled as close to the fire as we could get. I had gone out, in wolf morph, and dragged as much wood as I could back to the cave. I hoped it would be enough to last the night. And fortunately, I had retrieved my clothes after the morphing.

Night had fallen. The orange glow of the fire lit the low roof of the cave. But it didn't reach out into the dark woods beyond.

"My parents will be totally frantic," I said.

"Mine, too," Karen said.

"I didn't know Yeerks had parents."

Karen poked the fire with a stick, pushing an unburned bit of wood into the glowing centre. "I see you've given up pretending. That's good. It gets boring after a while when someone sticks to an obvious lie. And yes, we have parents, although it's very different than it is with you humans."

It was the first time she'd called me a human instead of an Andalite. I guess I looked surprised.

"Yes, I know you're human. We don't know how to duplicate Andalite morphing technology, but we do understand parts of it. We know about the two-hour limit. And we know that you can't morph straight from one morph to another. You have to pass through your own, natural body first. You're human, all right. I guess you wouldn't want to tell me how you managed to acquire Andalite morphing technology?"

I looked at her curious face. Her very human

face. Her little girl face. I knew what lived inside her head. I knew she would deliver me up to Visser Three the first chance she got.

If Marco or Rachel had been there beside me, I know what they'd have said: she can't be allowed to survive unless we can find a way to hold her for three days. That is when the Yeerk in her head would need to return to the Yeerk pool for nourishment. Tobias and Ax would have agreed. Jake, too, although it would have bothered him terribly.

They would all have been right.

"You're thinking about destroying me," Karen said.

I hesitated a moment. Then I said, "Yes."

She swallowed. "You thought about it before. Back at the river."

I nodded. "But you seemed pretty confident then. You were trying to goad me. I should have known you had a Dracon beam weapon. You wanted me to morph and try to kill you. In mid-morph you'd have stunned me."

Karen nodded. "That was the plan."

"So why didn't you use the Dracon beam on the bear that was chasing you?"

She laughed, a little embarrassed. "Pure panic, I'm afraid. That big bear came after me and I just forgot I had the weapon. Besides, you saw what a great shot I was with the leopard." She held up her hands. "I have little girl hands and little girl muscles. That Dracon beam is designed to be wielded by a Hork-Bajir. I could barely reach the trigger."

"And now you have no weapons at all," I said.

"No."

"I could morph the wolf and make short work out of you."

"But you won't."

"Why won't I?" I asked.

She shook her head slowly. "I don't know why."

"Me neither," I said.

For a while neither of us spoke. "There's plenty to drink," Karen said, nodding towards the rain that sheeted down across the cave entrance. "But we're going to get hungry."

"I could catch us a rabbit or something," I said. "But it would mean leaving you here alone."

"The leopard."

I nodded. "It won't attack a wolf directly. But it sees you as a small, helpless, wounded creature. Perfect prey."

"Yes, I suppose it does," she said bitterly. "I didn't want this body! I wanted a human body, but not a weak, innocent little child. This is what they assigned me."

I noted the word "innocent". What a strange word for a Yeerk to use.

"That's how it works? They tell you what body to infest?"

She nodded. "Yeah. It's my third host. I started out with a Gedd host, like most of us coming up through the ranks. I was a Hork-Bajir for a while — boring duty, mostly, interspersed with terrifying battles. Then I was assigned to Earth and a human host. Now it's your turn."

"My turn for what?"

Karen gestured towards the fire and around the cave. "We're stuck here. No food. Nothing to do but talk. I tell you my life story, you tell me yours."

"You could just be lying, making things up."

"So could you. You humans are not always honest."

I nodded. "That's true, I guess."

"So tell me. How do you come to have Andalite morphing technology?"

I shrugged. "It was given to me by a great Andalite warrior named Elfangor."

Karen's face grew dark at the mention of that name. "Elfangor," she spat.

"You've heard of him?"

Karen nodded. "Part of the time I was a Hork-Bajir I was in Visser Three's personal guard. The Visser was obsessed with Elfangor. Something personal between the two of them. I don't know what. But he hated Elfangor."

"I was there when Visser Three murdered him."

"Murder? No, it wasn't murder. We're at war with the Andalites. There's no *murder* in war."

"It was murder," I said. "Cold-blooded murder of a helpless person."

Karen leaned forward, her face glowing from the fire. "And that Hork-Bajir whose throat you removed. Was he helpless, too?"

I jumped up. "Don't you compare what your people do with what *we* do. You can't compare the attacker and the victim. You people started this war. And it's you invading my planet, not the other way around."

Karen jumped up, wincing at the pain in her ankle. "We have a right to live!"

"This isn't about you living!" I yelled. "It's about you enslaving other people."

"It's what we are," she yelled back. "We're parasites, you humans are predators. How many pigs and cows and chickens and sheep do you kill each year to survive? You think being a predator is morally superior to being a parasite? At least the host bodies we take remain alive. We don't kill them, cut them into pieces, and grill them over a charcoal fire in our gardens."

"We're not pigs," I said.

"Oh yes, you are," she said, her face distorted and twisted with contempt. "That's all you are to us. Oink, oink."

Chapter 12

We took turns staying awake and watching the cave entrance. It was very weird, really. We were deadly enemies to each other. If Karen — or at least the Yeerk in her head — got the chance, she would run to Visser Three and give me up.

The Visser would have me taken. He'd take me to the Yeerk pool that extended far beneath the school and the shopping mall. Hork-Bajir would drag me out on the long steel pier. They would force my head under the lead-coloured sludge.

I would kick and scream, but it wouldn't matter. My head would go below the surface. And one of the Yeerk slugs that swam there would rush to my ear. It would flatten itself and squeeze itself in through my ear canal.

The pain would be awful. But the pain would be nothing compared to the horror.

The Yeerk would slither and squirm around my brain. It would flatten itself over the high parts and sink down into the cracks and crevices.

And then it would open my mind like a book. It would see every memory. It would know every secret. It would know that I wet my bed once when I was six and that I was so embarrassed I threw the sheet away in the rubbish. It would know that I checked the wardrobe every night just in case someone was hiding there. It would know that I once cheated on a maths test and felt so bad I deliberately failed the next test to make up. It would know that I cared for Jake.

The Yeerk would open my eyes and turn them left and right. It would decide what to focus on.

It would move my arms and my hands. It would decide what to pick up or put down.

It would decide when I ate, when I slept, when I took a shower or washed my hair. It would dress me. It would talk to my mum and kiss my dad good night.

And all the while, I would be able to see, to hear, to know exactly what was going on. As the Yeerk inside my brain betrayed my friends, I would know. When Rachel and Marco and Tobias and Ax and Jake were hunted down, one by one, and killed or enslaved, I would be standing there, giving advice to the Yeerks. I would be helping to destroy my friends.

And I would be helpless.

That's what Karen had planned for me. A living death. It's what the Yeerks had planned for the entire world. They would enslave all who were useful, and annihilate everything and everyone else.

I poked the fire with a stick. Karen stirred in her sleep.

It would be so easy . . . I had the power. I had the power to destroy her before she destroyed me.

I should do it.

But I knew I wouldn't. Not now. Not tonight. Not in cold blood. Life was sacred. Even the life of an enemy.

But how about the lives of my friends? Weren't their lives even more sacred?

Karen woke up. She yawned and looked around with that stupid-just-woke-up expression. "Is it time for me to take over?"

"I guess so," I said. "We're low on wood, so don't build the fire too high. If you see anything, yell."

I rolled on to my side facing away from her. I was sure I'd never sleep. But I did.

I slept and I dreamed.

ScreeEEEET! ScreeEEEEET! ScreeEEEET!

Twenty human-Controllers stood waiting, armed with rifles and shotguns and automatic weapons.

Behind them stood two dozen Hork-Bajir warriors.

We were trapped. We'd sneaked into the building to retrieve the Pemalite crystal. The crystal would free the Chee from their programming. The programming that forbade them ever to harm a living creature.

With the crystal, we could turn the powerful Chee into allies against the Yeerks.

Erek the Chee stood just outside the building. I could see him through the plate glass. If we could find a way to give him the crystal, maybe he could help.

And then in my dream, just as it had happened in reality, everything exploded into violence. Hork-Bajir leaped, slashing. And we fought.

We fought and fought. And we lost ground, and lost ground, and lost. . .

Until, far off, I seemed to hear shattering glass. And suddenly, there was Erek. The hologram that disguised him as a normal human kid was gone, too.

He was his own true self: an android of metallic grey and pearl white.

What happened next I have tried to forget. I had seen battles. This was no battle. This was slaughter.

I woke up, crying, with an echo of Erek's

bitter sobs in my head.

"You were yelling in your sleep," Karen said.

"Was I?"

She laughed. "You were yelling, 'No! No!' That kind of thing. Bad dream, I guess?"

"Bad memory," I said.

"Sounded like a battle," she said. "From some of what you were saying. But hey, here you are alive, right? So you must have won."

"Winning doesn't make it less terrible."

She snorted derisively, like I'd made a joke. "Of course it does. Don't pretend with me. I know humans. I know that you love conquest as much as any Yeerk."

"Not all of us."

"Oh, I see. So you have morals. You feel bad when you destroy an enemy." She said it with heavy sarcasm.

"Yes, I feel bad. Most humans do. Anyway, I do."

"Lies," she said, yawning. "More human lies."

"Karen?"

"What?"

"If that's all true, why have I let you live?"

She looked at me, and I saw her green eyes flicker for just a moment as doubt entered her thoughts.

She closed her eyes and did not answer.

Chapter 13

It rained all through the night till four or five AM. But when we stepped outside into the morning, the sun was coming up in a brilliant, clear blue sky.

Water still dripped down from leaves and pine needles. The ground was still soft and mushy. The rocks glistened and sparkled.

Karen pushed past me. She limped over to the spot where she'd dropped the Dracon beam. She began scrabbling around in the bushes on her hands and knees.

"You took it! You came out here while I was asleep and took it!"

I shook my head. "It was raining hard all night. We're on a slope. Maybe it was carried off down the hill. Or maybe the leopard took it."

I meant that last part as a joke. But Karen's head jerked around towards me, her expression intense and fearful. "You think this is funny?"

I shrugged. "You weren't going to use it on me, anyway," I said. "You don't need to."

"That's not the problem," she said. "We are issued weapons. We aren't supposed to lose them. The punishment for losing them is . . . is very painful. I shouldn't have been carrying it — I'm on an unauthorized mission. That will double my punishment."

She looked very old, staring down hopelessly at the spot where the Dracon beam had fallen. It was easy to see that run-off from the rainstorm had rushed down across that area. The ground was smooth and cut with gullies.

"Probably down in the river by now," I said. With her ankle, now swollen to three times its normal size, there was no way Karen could climb down there.

Karen looked lost and confused. "I can't go back without it," she said. "It will mean facing Sub-Visser Nineteen."

"Your boss?"

"Yes. My commander. I don't suppose you'd help me look for it?"

I shook my head. "No. Not a chance."

Karen laughed bitterly. "Well, they'll go easy on me when I bring you in."

"Maybe they'll give me to you," I said.

"Make me your host body."

"No thanks, I don't want any more young female human hosts. Too weak. Too emotional. Their heads too filled up with. . ." She broke off.

I waited for her to say more. But she didn't. She just set her crutch and started walking with a determined, if painful step.

I fell in behind her.

Too emotional? Their heads too filled up with . . . With what?

Was it possible the Yeerk inside Karen's head was bothered by Karen's thoughts? By her emotions?

I felt a tingling sensation up and down the back of my neck. Was there another way to deal with Karen? Was it possible that the Yeerk felt some doubts about what it was doing? Was it even possible, or was I just grasping at straws?

Could a Yeerk be turned around? Could a Yeerk be made to see that what it was doing was wrong?

I took a deep breath and began to follow the hobbling Controller. How? How to reach the Yeerk inside her?

"So," I said. "Looks like we have a long walk ahead of us. All day, if we're going in the right direction. Maybe more than one day, if we're going the wrong way."

"I'm starving," she muttered.

"How do you feel about mushrooms?"

"What?"

"Mushrooms. See? Over there, by that fallen log. You have to be careful, of course, because a lot of mushrooms are poisonous. But I did a paper for Life Sciences class last year. All about wild mushrooms. Those are edible."

"I'm not eating raw mushrooms. They're gross." She had fallen back into her character as a little girl. It was so strange. She was both a little girl and a full-grown Yeerk.

"Well, I'm going to get some. You may change your mind."

I tromped over and began very carefully choosing from among the mushrooms that had sprouted up during the rain. I squatted comfortably. "So, Karen, or whatever your Yeerk name is, tell me about your life. I know you don't like your commander. That's about it?"

"What's your game, human?" she sneered. "You save me, you guide me, now you feed me? What are you trying to prove?"

I lifted a pair of mushrooms each the size of my fist and stuffed them in my pockets. "It bothers you, doesn't it?"

"What bothers me?"

"It bothers you when your victims don't hate you."

She let out a harsh, barking laugh. She started to say something. Then she started to say something else. She ended up saying nothing.

I stood up and handed her a mushroom. "Here. You can eat it now or you can wait. We may find some nice green onions or even some edible flowers to go with it. Practically a salad."

"You think you understand me? You don't. Nothing bothers me," Karen said harshly.

"It doesn't bother you that you've enslaved a child?"

"Slavery is a human concept."

"OK. Then forget that. How about this: does it bother you when you hear Karen — the real Karen — crying inside your mind? Does it bother you when you're with her mother and Karen wants so badly to talk to her mum, just to tell her she loves her? Just to say, 'I love you, Mum,' and she can't even say that? Does it bother you then?"

Karen jerked like I'd slapped her. "You don't know what you're talking about!" she cried.

"Oh, don't I?" I said. "Let me ask Karen. Let me talk to Karen and ask her."

"This human host has no secrets from me," she said. "I know what she thinks."

"And feels," I added.

"And *feels*!" she said defiantly. "She hates me, OK? Does that make you feel superior? She hates me. She wants me dead. She sits there in the back of my mind and imagines me being tortured, dying a slow, screaming death! That's what she feels. Hate! Hate! Hate!"

The trees seemed to reverberate with the sound of her screaming voice. The birds fell silent.

I shook my head. "Let me speak to her. Let's ask her if she hates you."

"Shut up."

I smiled. "It works both ways, doesn't it? You can feel her emotions, but she can feel yours, as well. Is that it? She knows what's going on inside your mind. So what is it she really feels towards you? It's not hate."

"Shut up," Karen muttered again. She began to walk again, wincing with each step.

"It's pity, isn't it? She feels sorry for you."

Karen walked a few more steps. Over her shoulder and in a voice as cold as ice she said, "Let's see how much pity you feel after I've turned you over to Visser Three, Cassie. Let's see how well you control the hate when you are nothing but a helpless puppet."

Chapter 14

We didn't move very fast with Karen's bad ankle. It gave me a chance to look around.

"Look! Deer!" I said. I crouched down and Karen sank on to a log, grateful to take a rest.

"It's a mother and fawn," I said. "Look how alert she is. She smells us."

"Bambi," Karen muttered under her breath.

"Yeah," I said. "I loved that movie."

"This human . . . this host body of mine, it . . . she loved it, too. It was her favourite video-tape when she was younger. You humans make everything sentimental. It's an animal. So what?"

I shrugged. "To tell you the truth, I've been feeling that way myself lately."

I stood up and the two deer scampered away, showing us their tails.

"I thought you cared about animals."

"I did. I mean, I do. It's just lately . . . I don't know. Things have been confusing for me lately. Normal stuff like school or my family or even the animals I take care of, it's all started to seem boring or something."

Karen nodded. "Of course."

"What do you mean, 'Of course'?"

"I mean, look at what you do, who you are, what you experience. You fight. You kill. You have power and you use it. Of course that's more interesting than your old, normal life."

I shook my head and munched some of the mushroom I'd picked. "That's not it. I mean . . . I don't know what it is."

Karen laughed. "You were just an average, everyday kid, weren't you? Before you got the morphing power."

"Pretty much," I said.

"Now when you're morphing, or when you're in battle, you feel so alive! So vividly alive! Normal life seems boring now."

"Is that what being in a fight is like to you?" I asked. "Not to me. I hate it. I've just got all confused. How can I go around doing the things I do and still believe that life is sacred? That *every* life is sacred? Sometimes I'm a predator. Sometimes I'm prey. I don't know . . . it's confusing."

For a while, Karen said nothing. Then, like it

wasn't important, she said, "We have people like you, too."

"People like me?"

"Sure. Yeerks who oppose the wars, who feel it's wrong to take unwilling hosts."

I was so stunned I stopped walking. "What? There are Yeerks who are against all this?"

"Don't act so surprised. We aren't all the same." Her face took on a bitter, resentful expression. "See? You believe the Andalite propaganda about us. According to the Andalites, we're nothing but evil slugs. We don't deserve to be free, flying around the galaxy. We're just parasites."

"It was the Andalites who helped you achieve space flight," I said. "Seerow was his name, wasn't it? The Andalite who helped your people?"

Now it was Karen's turn to look surprised. "You know a lot." Her eyes narrowed. "You're not *all* humans, are you? There must be some Andalites with you."

"Without the Andalites, you'd still be trapped on your home world, isn't that true?"

"Yes. Without Seerow, we would be. He was the one good Andalite."

I smiled. "So there's at least one good Andalite."

"And many good Yeerks," she said.

"Maybe so."

Once again, neither of us said anything for a while as we walked on slowly. We emerged from the shade of the trees into a small meadow.

It was breathtaking. The rain had raised an explosion of flowers, all lifting their petals towards the sun. Golden and white and blue, all still glistening with morning dew.

"Do you know what life is like for us?" Karen asked. "In the Yeerk pool, I mean?"

"No."

"We are born with a hundred or more sisters and brothers. We don't hatch from eggs. And we aren't born the way mammals are born, either. Three Yeerks join together. They literally join together, with three bodies becoming one. Then that one body begins to fragment. It breaks up into smaller pieces, grubs they're called. Bit by bit the body disintegrates, and each grub that falls away becomes another Yeerk. Sometimes there are twins, two Yeerks from one grub. The parent-Yeerks die, of course."

She looked at me to see my reaction. "You aren't horrified? You aren't shocked?"

Actually, I was. "I've studied a lot of different animals, so I guess I'm kind of hard to shock."

Karen looked back at the meadow. "In our natural state, we have an excellent sense of smell. We have a good sense of touch. We can hear. We can communicate, using a language of ultrasonic squeaks. But we cannot see. We are blind, until we enter a host. Over the millennia we have moved up the evolutionary chain to more and more advanced hosts. Eventually, the Gedds became our basic host bodies.

"They are clumsy, slow creatures. But they have eyes. Oh, you can't imagine! You can't imagine the first time you enter a Gedd brain and seize control and suddenly, you are seeing! Seeing! Colours! Shapes! It's a miracle. To be blind and then to see!"

Suddenly she stooped down and snatched up a caterpillar from a leaf. "Do you see this? This is what I am, without a host body. Helpless! Weak! Blind!" She spun and pointed at the meadow. "Do you see those flowers? Do you see the sunlight? Do you see the birds flying? You hate me for wanting that? You hate me because I won't spend my life blind? You hate me because I won't spend my life swimming endlessly in a sea of sludge, while humans like you live in a world of indescribable beauty?"

She put the caterpillar down gently on its leaf.

"Most of you humans don't even know what you have. You have the most beautiful planet in the galaxy. No other place is so alive. In no other place are there so many trees, so many flowers, so many amazing creatures. You live in a palace. You live in paradise, and you hate me for wanting to live there, too."

77

"I don't hate you."

She ignored me. She was talking for herself now. "What choice do we have? Back to the Yeerk pools? Back to our home planet, with Andalite Dome ships in orbit above us, waiting for one of us to try and rise from the sludge, then blow us apart? Leave the universe to the almighty Andalites and the species they happen to like?"

Karen gave me a bleak, hard look. "There are those of us who wish it could be another way. That there was some middle choice between being slugs beneath the Andalite hooves, and being . . . and being. . ."

"Slave masters?" I suggested.

I expected her to yell at me. Instead she put her face close to mine. Her voice was low. Her green eyes so enormous I almost felt I could see through them to the Yeerk inside. "What would you do, Cassie? What would you do, if you were one of us? Would you live your life as a blind, helpless slug?"

I didn't have an answer. Instead I looked away.

A chance look.

Brown and black! Moving fast!

"Aaaahhh!" I screamed.

The leopard took two liquid, silent steps and with the third step, opened its killing jaws, aiming for Karen's throat.

Chapter 15

The leopard flew.

Karen never even had time to react. Neither did I.

But someone *did.*

It happened almost too fast to see. A blur of grey hurtled down from the sky. It hit the blur of brown and black.

A flash of talons, bright red blood welling around the leopard's eyes.

"Rrrooowwwrr!" the leopard snarled.

But it hit Karen, just the same. Down she went. I lunged towards the leopard.

Wham! It hit me with the back of one paw, as cool and calm as Jackie Chan. It was like being slammed by a hammer. I went down hard.

"Aaaahhhh! Help!" Karen screamed.

The osprey fluttered up a few metres, then came down again in a second attack. It raked the leopard's face, but this time the leopard struck back.

With a crumpling sound, the osprey was knocked down. It lay jerking and heaving in the dirt.

I had already started morphing, but it was too late. The leopard opened its jaws. Karen, on her back and screaming, kicked wildly at its face.

The leopard chomped her leg. Its jaws closed right over the splint of sticks. Karen screamed, in pain this time.

The leopard looked around, coolly surveying the situation. It could smell the dangerous wolf smell already coming from me. It decided maybe this was not the place to eat its prey.

The leopard began to drag Karen away. It still held her ankle and dragged her along backwards across the dirt and leaves and pine needles.

"Help me! Help me, Cassie! I'll let you go, I swear! Help me!"

I staggered after her on bandy, half-wolf legs, lumbering clumsily and slowly, half-human, half-wolf.

"Help me! Help me! Aarrggghh!"

I looked at Marco. Because, of course, he was the osprey. He was fluttering weakly and starting to stand up. He was also starting to demorph. He'd be OK. But Karen would not be OK. As soon as the leopard felt safe it would apply the killing bite: to the throat, to the back of the neck, or even to the head itself.

I was mostly wolf now. But would the leopard back down? The last time, I'd scared it away before it got to Karen. Now it would be defending its "kill".

And I had a bad feeling about fighting a leopard one-on-one.

I bounded forwards, letting out a threatening growl.

The leopard turned, keeping Karen's leg twisted in its mouth. It stared at me with curious yellow eyes.

We were each about seventy-five kilogrammes. We each had powerful jaws. Each of us was fast. I had an armour of thick fur around my neck to ward off bites. But the leopard's teeth were much longer than mine. And it had four deadly paws, each armed with hooked, ripping, razor-sharp claws.

I felt a terrible sinking sensation. One-on-one, in a fight to the death, I would lose.

We stood staring at each other, just four metres apart.

Karen lay on her side, shaking in terror, her face contorted by pain.

"Help me," she moaned pitifully. "Don't let him eat me."

I was shocked. I knew right then: the person begging for help was the real Karen. Not the Yeerk in her head.

At least if I charged, the leopard would have to let her go to fight me.

I advanced a few steps. The leopard opened his mouth and spat out Karen's leg. It bared its teeth, drawing its lips back in a hideous snarl.

It screamed a threat: "Hhhheeerrrooowwwrr!"

It wasn't going to just walk away this time. It had tasted the blood of its prey. It wasn't going to walk away without a fight.

Karen began to crawl slowly away, sobbing.

The leopard watched me. With senses so alert they made the air tingle with electricity, it watched me, waiting, ready.

<Marco, if you can hear me, I am gonna need help,> I said.

I charged.

It was like running into a tornado. I thought the wolf was fast. It wasn't. I'd been slashed in half a dozen places while I was still snapping at the air with my jaws.

Slash!

Slash!

Slash!

I backed away, bleeding, shocked. The leopard's speed was at a whole different level. And now the leopard knew. It *knew* it could beat me.

"Hhhheeerrrooowwwrr!" the leopard snarled, with a note of triumph in its voice. Snarling, it bared its ten-centimetre teeth.

It was simple. I could turn and run, and the leopard would let me go. Or I could stay and fight.

I've fought before. I've fought Hork-Bajir. But I've never been more afraid of any creature. The leopard wasn't just quick. It was quick, with perfect accuracy and terrifying grace. It was fast while looking almost lazy. It was like a supernatural thing. Like it existed outside of my whole notion of time.

I was a big, clunky thing made out of sticks and nails. The leopard was made of mercury. It was liquid metal.

Was I insane? Was I going to die to save a Yeerk who would destroy me herself? It made no sense. It was absurd. No one but a fool would even think of it.

No, not to save the Yeerk, a voice in my head said. *To save Karen, a scared little girl.*

Don't be an idiot! There was no Karen, not any more. Karen was just a puppet of the Yeerk.

You don't risk your life to save your enemies. You protect your friends and destroy your enemies. That was life. *That* was reality. Basic survival of the fittest: protect yourself first, protect your own family and tribe second. Protect your enemies *never*.

Walk away, Cassie, I told myself. The leopard will be quick about it. One bite and it will be all over for Karen and the Yeerk in her head. One bite and the threat will be gone. One bite and the secret of the Animorphs will be safe.

Die for your enemy?

No, walk away.

I stood there, poised, frozen, unable to decide.

And then I saw the leopard's malevolent gaze waver. It focused up and behind me.

I sniffed the air and knew what had happened.

<Run away, little kitty,> Marco said. <You may be able to take on a wolf, and you may be able to take on a gorilla, but you can't take on both of us.>

The light in the leopard's eyes went dull. The calculation had changed: the odds were too great now.

It turned and walked slowly away. It had backed down twice now. And I had the feeling the leopard didn't like losing.

It stopped near a tall fir tree and looked back over its shoulder. It stared at me with its yellow eyes. Of course it couldn't talk, but I knew what it was saying: *next time the little one is mine.*

Chapter 16

<How's *that* for a last minute rescue?> Marco crowed. <I *am* the cavalry. I *am* the Police. Now all we have to do is figure out how to explain to that little girl that a gorilla and a wolf are working together.>

The "little girl" was clutching her ankle and writhing in pain. I began to demorph.

<Hey! Hey! What are you doing, Cassie? You can't demorph in front of that girl!>

<I have to. She needs help.>

<So run off into the bushes, out of sight. Then come back. She's just a kid. You can come up with some story to explain it. She was probably too scared from the leopard to even track on what you and I were doing.>

I continued demorphing. <Marco, she

already knows.>

<What do you mean, she already knows?> Marco said, all humour and joking gone from his voice.

I made the transition to mostly human. "I mean, she knows."

<Oh, great, Cassie!> he sighed. <OK, well, she's just a kid. Who's gonna believe her if she starts ranting and raving about some girl who turned into a wolf?>

I knelt in front of Karen and began unwrapping the splint I'd made around her ankle.

"Listen to me," I said in a low whisper I hoped only Karen would hear. "Don't tell him what you are. Not if you want to live."

But Marco is not a fool. He could see that I was whispering. And Karen was in such pain I wasn't sure she even understood.

<I have an idea,> Marco said. <How about telling me what's going on? You disappear, your parents are both losing their minds from worry. We all go looking for you, and now, here you are, whispering to this girl.>

I was human again, so I couldn't answer him in thought-speak. It gave me a little time to think about what I should tell him.

<Ah. OK. Tell you what. I'll go "bye-bye" for a couple of seconds and come back as my own cute, lovable self.>

Marco lumbered away, a massive, powerful

gorilla with shoulders that looked like they'd been built by Mack trucks.

"He'll be back in a few seconds," I hissed to Karen as I tore strips of cloth from my morphing outfit to clean her wound. "If he finds out what you are, he might . . . he might not see things the way I do."

Karen grimaced in pain, but the Yeerk in her head was still alert and sharp. "A monkey morph? How's he going to hurt me with that?"

"You idiot," I snapped, "that gorilla morph could rip a tree out of the ground and play baseball with you as the ball."

"Sorry," she muttered. "The only things I know about Earth creatures are what the host brain knows. She thinks he looks like Curious George."

"He's curious, all right. And smart. And he doesn't like Yeerks. And in that morph he could stuff you into the nearest gopher hole, so listen to me!"

"Why are you protecting me from him? You weren't so sure about saving me from the leopard, were you?"

I didn't answer. Instead I focused on cleaning the wound. It wasn't easy, and it was almost useless. The bite marks didn't go deep because the wood splint had stopped them. But they were sure to become infected eventually. And there could be crushed blood vessels below the surface that I couldn't even see.

"How does it look?" she asked.

"I don't know. It might become infected. It could even lead to gangrene."

"What's gangrene?"

"Putrefied flesh," I said harshly. "It could mean the foot will have to be amputated if it goes on too long. Maybe more of the leg."

To my surprise, Karen laughed. "That would be just perfect. I'd not only be stuck in a little girl host body, I'd be stuck in a *crippled* little girl."

"She's already crippled," I said. "What do you think you've done to her? She's already lost both her legs, and her arms and eyes and voice as well."

She looked up at me with her startling green eyes. "You hate me so much? Why don't you just finish me off?"

"Because I can't destroy you without destroying the girl," I said.

She shook her head. "No. No, that's not all there is to it." Suddenly she burst out laughing. "Ah, hah, hah, hah! Amazing! I just figured it out! You're trying to turn me. You're trying to get me to turn against my own side."

"I'm trying to save you," I whispered.

Karen snorted. "You want to make peace, don't you? You want to find a way to stop us without having to get your hands dirty. You want to defeat us . . . without having to kill us. It's almost sweet. It *is* sweet. Sweet and naive and foolish and utterly, utterly futile."

<I agree.>

I turned and saw Marco. Only he was in his osprey morph again, sitting seven metres above us in a tree.

Ospreys, like all birds of prey, have amazing eyesight. But what many people don't know is that they also have very excellent hearing.

<I absolutely agree,> Marco said, his thought-speak voice vibrating with suppressed rage. <There's no peace with parasites. You don't turn them around. You bury them.>

Chapter 17

"There! There you have it!" Karen cried, pointing triumphantly at Marco. "Kill! Kill, he cries. Kill the parasite! Kill the Yeerk. Now where is your human morality? Now tell me again, Cassie, how you humans and your Andalite friends are better than we are!"

<We don't crawl into people's brains and make them slaves,> Marco said. He flapped down from the tree to the ground and began to demorph.

"Of course not. You're predators. So you think being a predator is fine. Well, we think being parasites is fine," Karen said, smirking. "Your morality is real simple. Anything humans do is OK, anything Yeerks do is wrong."

Marco was mostly human now. Human

enough to speak and to jab his finger angrily at Karen. "Hey, Slug-girl, we didn't start this fight, you did. We didn't go to the Yeerk planet and start killing Yeerks. You started this war."

"Who started the war between humans and cows? Or humans and pigs? Or humans and chickens?" Karen demanded, laughing derisively. "Cows weren't eating humans, were they?"

"Hey, we're not cows," Marco snapped. "You can't compare what you do to humans with what we do to cows."

"Sure I can. You're our *meat*!" Karen said.

It was a harsh, spitting, evil statement. It seemed even more so coming from a little girl's mouth.

She and Marco stood face to face, glaring. I felt as if I couldn't breathe. Like I couldn't make my mind work.

"Cassie, we have no choice," Marco said. "She knows too much. We can't let her walk out of these woods alive."

"She's not just a Yeerk," I begged. "She's also a little girl."

"The little girl has gone," Marco said. "She's not in charge any more. That Yeerk piece of crap is."

"That's a funny thing for you to say, Marco. You, of all people," I said.

I was talking, talking like I knew what I was saying. But inside me was a storm. I felt like I was going to explode. I didn't know what to do!

His eyes flickered. "What are you talking about?"

"You know what I'm talking about, Marco. There's someone you know . . . someone close to you who is just like Karen."

Marco's mother is a Controller. Everyone, even Marco's dad, thinks she's dead. But we know that she is controlled by the Yeerk, Visser One.

"And she's not the only one. You and I have a close friend, Marco, whose brother is one of them."

Tom, Jake's brother, is also a Controller.

"So what are you telling me? We can't fight the Yeerks because they hide behind humans? What do we do, just give up? Look, Cassie, you're so worried about this Controller here, why don't you worry about all of us — you know who I mean. You think she and her fellow Yeerks will hesitate to destroy us?"

I felt the edge of panic rise a little higher. He was right. It was either Karen or the Animorphs. One or the other. Both could not survive. I couldn't go on pretending. I couldn't find an answer.

"I don't know," I muttered desperately. "I don't know."

Marco rolled his eyes. His opinion of me was obvious. It was OK: I agreed with him. I was a muddled, confused, foolish girl. I was sacrificing my friends . . . for what? I was selling out the entire human race . . . for what?

So I wouldn't have to see one lost little girl destroyed? So I wouldn't have to know that a Yeerk — yes, a Yeerk, with her own life and feelings and thoughts — was going to perish?

"I'll make it simple for you, Yeerk," Marco said. "You're going to die, that much we know. Now, you can leave that little girl and at least not take anyone else down with you, or . . . well, nothing personal, but you're not leaving this forest alive."

"No," Karen said simply. "You want to kill me? You have the power. But I'm not making it easy for you."

"OK," Marco said. He said it casually, like it was all no big deal to him. I knew better. I knew he was feeling the awful violence-sickness inside of him. But I also knew he would do it.

The three of us seemed frozen in time, no one ready to make the first move. The three of us just stood and stared and waited . . . no! Not the *three* of us.

"Wait!" I cried. "There's another person here who should have a chance to speak."

Marco raised an eyebrow.

I looked at Karen. "I want to hear from the *real* Karen. The human little girl."

Karen laughed. "Don't be an idiot. You

93

should know I can sound exactly like Karen if I want to. You'd never know for sure."

"I would if you weren't in her," I said. I began to morph, as fast as I could, back into the wolf.

"Yeah, that's what I'll do," the Controller jeered. "I'll just leave my host body and lie on the ground so your murderous predator friend here can—"

"Cassie, what are you doing?" Marco demanded. He'd noticed that I was morphing.

<I'm giving this Controller a place to go, so we can hear from Karen.>

With my half-hands, half-paws, I grabbed Karen's head and pulled it to me. I pressed her ear against mine.

"Nooooo!" Marco screamed.

But there was nothing he could do to stop me. I was a wolf. He was a human. Already I could feel the tingling touch in my ear.

"What are you doing?!" Marco yelled. "Are you insane? What are you doing?"

I didn't have an answer. I didn't know the answer. I was beyond logic and reason now. I just didn't want to have to hurt anyone or anything.

That was all: I just didn't want to hurt. . .

Marco began to morph back to osprey. He'd understood instantly what I hadn't even thought about: the Yeerk that was entering my brain would be able to use my morphing power. If he stayed in human form, the Yeerk, using my morphing power, might attack him.

"I'm going to get the others," Marco said, seething with fury. "You're a fool, Cassie. Now it's not the little girl who may have to die. It's *you*."

Chapter 18

I felt the start of an awful pain in my ear. But the Yeerk secreted a chemical that made my ear go numb. And then I felt it pushing its way through my ear canal the way you still kind of feel the dentist's drill even after the injection.

I felt the first touch of the Yeerk on my mind. There was no pain now. There was just a feeling of . . . I don't know how to describe it. A feeling that I was being paralysed, a little at a time.

It touched my brain, and all at once I realized I could no longer move my right leg.

It reached further, and my hands were no longer mine.

It reached further, and the hunger I'd felt was now someone else's hunger.

It reached further and further, sliding into

the crevices. Slithering between the cauliflower contours of the gelatinous grey mass that was my brain.

I looked at Karen. The simple, human Karen. She was crying.

"I want to go home," she sobbed.

And then my eyes moved and looked away. They focused on Marco as he flapped his grey and white wings and rose from the ground.

I hadn't moved my eyes.

It was all over so quickly. So quickly I lost all control of my own body.

And then the Yeerk opened my memory. It was easy as any person reading a book. I felt my secrets, all my little shames and embarrassments, lying open for the Yeerk to inspect, to laugh at.

But at the same time, parts of her mind seemed to soak into my consciousness. I could see her. Not as well as she could see me, because I could not control which of her memories I looked at. But just the same, the Yeerk's mind seemed to blur into mine.

I was there, in the Yeerk pool, blind, swimming. I had a name and a designation: I was Aftran-Nine-Four-Two of the Hett Simplat pool.

I was there, in Aftran's memories, opening Gedd eyes for the first time and seeing colour! Oh, the shock! Oh, the glory of it! Even second-hand, even from so long ago, the beauty of colour seen for the first time was overwhelming.

I was there when the Yeerk first felt its Hork-Bajir host. Felt the grace and power that the Gedd would never have.

I was there when the new Hork-Bajir-Controller was in its first blade fight. The fear it had felt!

And after the battle, after the next battle, and the next, and the next, some other memory grew and grew. A memory of sadness. A memory of regret.

Aftran was saddened by the battles.

Then the human morph. Karen.

Aftran had volunteered for the duty. She had wanted out of the Hork-Bajir body. She wanted out of the war. What could be a safer, more peaceful host than a little, human girl?

The assignment was to watch her father. He was the billionaire owner of UniBank. Being close to him gave Aftran access to all sorts of information and vast amounts of useful cash. The Yeerks wanted to make the father a Controller, but hadn't been able to yet. So Karen had been taken, and made into a Controller to watch the true target: her father.

Aftran had taken on the job to avoid having to kill. But her pool-brother, Estril, had stayed on as a Hork-Bajir. Estril had been acting as back-up security to a meeting of The Sharing. A nothing job. No problem. Stay aboard a shielded ship, just in case. . .

The "just in case" had been the battle. And I saw, with Aftran's memory, the image of a wolf, teeth bared in a vicious snarl. . .

Me.

And now Aftran opened that very memory. I could feel her absorbing my crystal clear images: the moment when I lunged for the Hork-Bajir's throat and heard Jake yell, <OK, they've had it, back away! Back away!>

<His name was Estril-Seven-Three-One, of the Hett Simplat pool,> Aftran said to me.

<Yes,> I said. And as the guilt welled up inside me, I could tell that Aftran was watching the emotion, solemnly curious.

Now the Yeerk opened the secret I had guarded for months. She yelped in surprise. <Just five human children and an Andalite *aristh*?!> She laughed. <The entire Yeerk invasion force is in an uproar because of five human children and an Andalite cadet?>

One by one she looked inside the memories I had formed since becoming an Animorph.

She saw the construction site where Elfangor's fighter had crash-landed.

She saw the moment when I learned that Tobias was trapped for ever in hawk morph.

She saw the first time I ever morphed a dolphin, the amazing, giddy joy of it, and I swear she laughed inside my head, enjoying the memory, too.

She saw that Jake's brother Tom was a Controller, that the leader of the Animorphs lived under the same roof with a Yeerk.

She saw that Marco's mother was Visser One and the fact that it was Visser One who had freed us from Visser Three's clutches for her own evil reasons.

<Politics and power,> Aftran sneered. <The Vissers spend more time attacking each other than they spend attacking our enemies. All they care about is their own power.>

She saw the hidden, underground park where the Chee care for the stray dogs that remind them of their long-dead masters.

She saw, as I had seen, through the eyes of the wolf, the dolphin, the skunk, the horse, the osprey, even the Tyrannosaurus. She experienced the distorted, eerie universe of the fly, the cockroach, the flea, the ant.

And she dwelled at length on the termite. As she opened that memory, it was like being back there again, deep in the tiny tunnels within rotted wood. A lightless, sightless, scent-defined world of mindless automatons.

She saw me destroy the termite queen.

<You felt guilty for killing an insect?> she marvelled.

She discovered, through me, the secret of

Zone 91 and laughed and laughed at that. <An Andalite portable toilet! Hah-hah-hah! Visser Three is obsessed with discovering the secret of Zone ninety-one.>

And she came, at last, back again to the last few days. Back to now. Back to where she could watch herself through my eyes. To feel my own complicated mix of emotions.

Then there was silence, and no more memories opened. Not for a long time. And Aftran's mind went away, closed off by itself.

I tried moving my eyes, but they were still beyond my control. I wanted to scream. It was like being paralysed. I was completely powerless. Completely.

I sat there, waiting. Unable to move, unable even to control my own memory. All that was left to me were my own emotions.

And those . . . I couldn't make sense of those. All I knew for sure was that I had betrayed everyone I cared about. Jake. Rachel. Tobias. Ax. Marco.

And then, I felt Aftran opening a specific memory. I felt her causing me to focus and concentrate.

As she herself aimed my eyes, I saw the grey, feather patterns begin to appear on my skin, like drawings that slowly came to life.

The Yeerk spread my wings. And she flew.

Chapter 19

Up we flew, up from the pine-needle-covered floor of the forest. Up, up through the tree-tops. Up into brilliant sunlight.

The osprey's eyes scanned the horizon, from the distant mountains, to the sea, now just a kilometre away, down to the farms and roads and petrol stations and Dairy Queens no more than five kilometres distant.

It would be child's play for the Yeerk to fly to the nearest petrol station, demorph, and call his superiors. Then it would all be over.

Jake would be seized, probably by Tom himself. Rachel would be taken on her way to the mall. Marco, Ax, Tobias, one by one. They would each be dragged, unwilling, crying, screaming, begging, or perhaps with whatever dignity they could hold on to. Down, down into the Yeerk pool.

And there, stunned unconscious to keep them from morphing, they would have their heads shoved down into the sludge of the Yeerk pool.

And at that moment, their freedom would die. And perhaps the last, best hope of humanity would die as well.

My fault.

All my fault.

I was a fool. I was a coward. I'd been unwilling to do the hard, brutal, necessary thing. Instead I'd followed . . . what? A wish? An instinct? A pathetic hope?

<To be like this,> the Yeerk said dreamily in my head. <Oh, to be like this. To fly. All alone, up here in the sky! To have these eyes. I can see everything! Everything down to the tiniest blade of grass.>

I waited for Aftran to head towards civilization. But she didn't. She circled. Unsure. I could hear and feel her doubts.

But then, down below, threading their way through the trees, a dozen men in state police uniforms. They were moving along the river. Glancing left, the osprey's eyes saw Karen, still sitting hunched on a rock.

Several thousand metres of dense forest separated the men from the girl.

<A rescue party,> I thought. <Of course. I'm missing. Karen is missing. There will be a massive search under way.>

<Yes, there probably is,> Aftran agreed. <But those aren't normal rescuers. They are Controllers. I know some of them. They aren't looking for you, they're looking for me. They will expect me to be in Karen. If they find her, they'll know I've made you my host. They'll ask why.>

Was Aftran anxious? Afraid? Why?

She moved the osprey's head and swept the horizon anxiously. And that's when I saw the birds. They were far off, even for osprey vision, but one, the largest, was definitely a bald eagle. And the other birds flying with it were not eagles.

I could guess what the other birds were: a peregrine falcon, a northern harrier, another osprey, and, of course, a red-tailed hawk.

I tried to shut the knowledge off from Aftran, but she knew as soon as I knew.

<So. Your friends are coming. To rescue you? Or to kill you?>

<To kill you,> I told the Yeerk. <They'll hold me until you starve from lack of Kandrona rays.>

I could tell Aftran was shocked. <You know about Kandrona rays! Of course, I see it now. I haven't had time to open all your memories.>

<Your people will find Karen,> I said. <When they find she's no longer a Controller, they'll kill

her, won't they? They can't allow her to go around telling what she knows. They'll kill that little girl.>

<And your friends will kill me!> Aftran said. <Do you know what it's like to die of Kandrona starvation? Do you know what kind of agony it is?>

<Then let's put an end to the killing!> I cried. <Your side, my side. The Animorphs will be here soon. They've seen me. There will be a battle. Some of those Controllers down there on the ground will die! Some of my friends may die! Karen may die! You may die! For what? For what?>

She laughed bitterly. <You think we can make peace between human and Yeerk and Andalite? Don't be stupid.>

<No, I don't think we can make peace between all humans and all Yeerks and all Andalites. But you and I can have peace. One Yeerk, one human.>

Aftran said nothing. But I could hear echoes of her thought. Back to the Yeerk pool. To hide among the other Yeerks. To try and disappear in the mass of slugs. To leave her host and never return.

Never to see again. Never to see blue, green, red. Never again to see the sun. Any sun.

Why? So some little human girl with green eyes could be free?

<Do you know what you're asking me to do?> Aftran demanded.

<Yes,> I said.

<And if you were me?>

I hesitated. <I can't answer that. I'm not you.>

But Aftran opened my brain again, flipping through pages of memory, listening to my instincts, absorbing my beliefs.

<You believe you would sacrifice anything to save Karen,> Aftran said. <That's what you believe. You believe if you were me, you would make the sacrifice.>

<But I'm not you,> I said again.

<Maybe you are,> she said coldly. <More than you think.>

Aftran turned in the warm, morning air and began flapping back towards Karen.

And that's when an echo of Aftran's thoughts bubbled up inside my own consciousness, and I felt the heart-freezing dread.

Chapter 20

We flew first over the heads of the Controllers. The human-Controllers disguised as state police.

<On the ground, there. Yaheen-Seven-Four-Seven, this is Aftran-Nine-Four-Two of the Hett Simplat pool. I know you can't see me. But listen to my warning: a group of five birds of prey is coming this way. They are the Andalite bandits in morph!>

I saw the human-Controllers looking around, puzzled at the sudden thought-speak, but also looking worried. They began to unlimber their guns.

<So much for peace,> I said bitterly. But then, I realized: she had said "Andalite bandits". Aftran had lied to her fellow Yeerks.

We landed beside Karen. She had managed to hobble and crawl into the meadow. She didn't realize it, but it had taken her a little farther from the searching Controllers.

It could take them hours to find her now. And possibly my own friends would be delayed, too, as the human-Controllers tried to attack them.

More battle. More violence. Pointless.

<Not pointless,> Aftran said, reading my thoughts as if they were her own.

The osprey came to rest within a metre or so of Karen. Karen had stopped crying. Now she gazed in wonder and confusion, as I . . . as Aftran . . . as *we* began to demorph.

The feathers melted away and flesh re-appeared. My eyes grew dim and human again. My hearing was clouded. My wings became arms and my talons grew to become legs.

Karen's face took on a look of defeat. She realized now who I was. And what was inside my head.

Karen tried to turn away, tried to run. But her ankle failed her instantly and down she went in the grass. Her hand clutched at a bundle of yellow wild flowers.

<Don't do this, Aftran,> I cried. <Stay in me, let her go!>

But as I watched, helpless inside my own body, I saw my own hands reach out and take Karen roughly.

She cried and beat at me with small fists, but my hands blocked her blows. My hands grabbed her head and held her ear against my own.

I wanted to cry, but I didn't control my own tears. I wanted to comfort her, but my voice was not mine.

I pressed Karen against me and held her tight, and the Yeerk named Aftran extended a slithering extrusion from my ear into Karen's.

It took a few minutes. Slowly, gradually, bit by bit, I felt myself regain control.

I could turn my eyes. I could move my legs. But Aftran retained control of my hands until she was almost entirely across, back inside Karen's head.

My hands! I controlled them. I pushed away, shoving Karen from me.

I saw the last of the Yeerk. The last of the slithering, grey slug shloop into Karen's head.

I sat down, suddenly too exhausted and dispirited to run or morph or even think. I just wanted to cry. I guess maybe I did. I don't know.

Karen's voice said, "Your friends or mine will find us soon, but not very soon, I think."

"What does it matter?" I asked.

"It matters that they not find us for two hours."

"What are you planning on doing?" I asked. I looked up and realized that Karen's green eyes were filled with tears. Karen's tears. But they only flowed because Aftran, the Yeerk, was crying.

"You tell me what you think I should do," Karen said harshly, despite the tears. "Andalites, humans, there's no difference: you're both smug, moralizing, superior races. You both live in beautiful worlds. You have hands and eyes and the freedom to move about wherever you like. And you hate us for wanting all those same things."

"We can't help what we are, any more than you can. We're born with eyes and hands and legs. You're born as . . . as what you are."

"Slugs!" Karen cried. "That's what you call us, isn't it? Slugs! Like some wet, slimy thing crawling across the pavement after it rains. Something you step on and say 'Eewww, gross!'"

"You're a Yeerk. I can't change that. You can't change it, either. All you can do is make other creatures into slaves so you can be more free. How can you justify making Karen a slave so you can be free? It's wrong. I don't care if you're human or Andalite or Yeerk, it's wrong."

Karen looked at me and nodded. "Yes. I know." She shrugged her shoulders and looked down at the ground. She bent down and raised a leaf so I could see it. Hanging from the bottom of the leaf was a caterpillar. It was maybe two centimetres long. It hung from the bottom of the leaf and was busy writhing out of its old skin. The old skin was gathered around the caterpillar like a sock that has fallen down your leg.

"This is what I am," Karen said. "A slug. A worm. What this little creature experiences is what I would experience if I didn't have a host body."

"I . . . I'm sorry," I said. It was all I could think of to say.

"You ask me to become this worm again. You ask a lot of me, Cassie the Animorph. You say we can make peace between us, just you and me and Karen. You say we can make a start. And then you ask me to give up everything, while you go on about your life, living amidst splendour and magnificence."

All I could do was to shake my head. I didn't even know what it meant. Was I denying what she said? No. It was the truth.

"So I ask you, Cassie," Karen said in a silky voice. "What will you give up, if I give up everything?"

"I . . . what can I. . ."

Karen carefully, gently placed the half-cocooned caterpillar in my hand. "Let its DNA flow into you, Cassie."

"No," I whispered.

"You ask me to pay a terrible price to make Karen free again. Will you pay the same price? Will you become this little creature? Will you stay in that morph for two hours while I stand guard?"

"But . . . I would be trapped permanently!" I cried.

"Yes. Just as I will be trapped permanently."

I couldn't breathe. My heart kept pounding really fast, then seemed to stop. I couldn't even see anything — just Karen's face and the caterpillar.

"It's a lot easier to tell someone else what they must do than to do it yourself, eh, Cassie?" Karen mocked.

"It's a trick," I whispered. "You'd trap me, then you'd just laugh and take off."

Karen shook her head. "You know better than that. You have morphing power. As a host body, you would be incredibly valuable. Visser Three is the only morph-capable Yeerk. Your body, along with the bodies of your friends? Unbelievably valuable. I would be the Yeerk who captured the Animorphs. They'd make me a sub-visser at the very least. I'd have it all: a great assignment, my choice of host bodies. Do you think I would deliberately trap a morph-capable body as a bug if I weren't sincere? I'm giving up *everything*! Will you give up *nothing*?"

I looked down at the caterpillar, squirming in my trembling hand.

I raised my eyes and looked around at the world. The trees. The grass. The sky. The flowers.

I had cared about nature all my life. And still I had not understood how magnificent it was until that moment.

To lose my parents. My friends. The entire world.

To save my parents. My friends. Maybe even the entire world.

I closed my eyes and began to focus. And the DNA of the caterpillar entered my blood.

Chapter 21

The caterpillar grew still. It stopped writhing. Most animals become calm and quiet while being acquired.

"Now do it," Karen said.

I wanted to argue. I wanted to say, "Forget it!" I could morph to the wolf instead and kill her. It would save my friends. It would save me.

But it wouldn't free the little girl named Karen from the Yeerk in her head. And it would just be more of the same: violence and brute force and another innocent victim.

I looked around me at all I was losing. And I focused my mind as I had done a hundred times before.

Slowly, the changes began. I am a fast morpher normally. Even Ax says so. But I was not hurrying now. I wanted to hold on to every last second of my life as a human.

But still the changes came.

My legs began to shrink. I was falling, falling towards the ground. Karen's face, which had been lower than mine, became level with mine, then higher than mine.

The ground rushed up towards me, pine needles thickening to become twigs, blades of grass looking like saplings. Karen's swollen, splinted ankle looked as thick as a redwood tree.

As my legs shrank, so did my arms. I stared down at them as they withered, twisting and curling like a paper that's been thrown on the edge of a fire. The fingers curled and disappeared.

My body was thickening, elongating. The trunk of my body was now huge compared to my arms and legs. And my head was getting smaller as well. My field of vision was distorted by the fact that my eyes were moving closer together.

Suddenly, all along my back, tiny sharp daggers sprouted — the spines of the caterpillar.

And all along my front, sets of minuscule legs began to emerge. It was beyond creepy. I looked like a Taxxon! Three pairs of little, sharp legs grew out of my chest. Four more sets of somewhat different-looking legs grew from my stomach. My own two legs melted together, and quite suddenly I was in the body of a worm.

I wanted to cry. Morphing is always terrifying. Morphing a new creature is the most terrifying thing. But morphing a hideous bug and knowing that you will spend the rest of your life in that body!

I felt a clenching, like someone was tightening a series of belts all up and down my body. I looked down and saw the puffy yellow and green flesh become a dozen segments. It was like those little snap-together plastic blocks babies play with.

I fell forward, helpless. It seemed like a long fall, but I was now no more than fifteen centimetres long and still shrinking.

I saw pine needles as big as telephone poles rush up at me. I saw a beetle walking by, looking as large as a dog. I saw a flash of colour — flowers all around, the sky, and Karen's green eyes. And then I saw nothing more.

I landed with a soft *poof*!

My rows of legs absorbed the slight shock. I could still sense vibration. I could feel my mouthparts moving. I knew that the caterpillar's extremely simple, basic mind was rising up within my own. It was urgent. In a hurry. Hunger? No, something else. Something it had to do.

I could fight the caterpillar mind. I could resist. But what would be the point?

Demorph! Demorph! I cried. *Don't do it!* I begged myself.

But now it was already too late. If I demorphed, Karen would know our deal was off. And I would be totally vulnerable as I slowly returned to human form.

I cried out silently, pleading, begging, screaming.

But there was no answer.

I was alone. I was more alone than any human being has ever been.

I abandoned myself to the caterpillar, and it began to climb the stalk of a flower it could not see.

Chapter 22

Jake

My name is Jake.

I was in my peregrine falcon morph searching for Cassie when Marco came rushing up, flapping at full speed.

<I found her,> he said. But his thought-speak voice was grim.

<What's happened?> I demanded.

<The short version? She's a Controller now. And if we don't haul butt we're dog food.>

I absorbed the sudden shock. No time for feeling scared for Cassie. I had to act. But we would need everyone together, and that would take time. We were spread out over thirty kilometres of forest.

Cassie's parents had started worrying when she didn't come back from supposedly fixing the water trough. Her mum had started calling all her friends, starting with Rachel. Her dad had gone out to where the trough was and found Cassie's favourite mare wandering around outside the fence, scratched up, wet, with its saddle over on one side.

Her dad knows wild animals. He found the bear tracks. He followed the horse and bear tracks until it got too dark to see.

They called the cops and the park service. A search was organized. But it's almost impossible for people to find a single person in over a hundred square kilometres of forest.

Rachel called me. I called the others. Marco said something he didn't really mean about Cassie not being an Animorph any more, so she wasn't our problem. Rachel knocked him on his butt.

Marco is my best friend, but there are times I admire Rachel's directness.

We spent the night in owl morphs, floating silently above the forest. Owls see blackest night like noon with a cloudless sky. But all we were seeing were the many little forest animals, and, occasionally, the search parties and their torches.

It was Marco who figured out that we were making a mistake. Looking with eyes wasn't the only way. He morphed to wolf and used his incredible sense of smell to follow the scent of

119

the mare to the edge of the river. We found a torn strip of fabric hanging from a bramble bush.

Cassie had gone into the river.

Then we overheard some of the searchers talking. It wasn't just Cassie who was missing now. There was a little girl named Karen.

When the sun came up we switched to bird-of-prey morphs. And we focused on following the course of the river. To tell you the truth, we were mostly looking for a body lying in the water. I mean, of course we still hoped she was alive. But we knew Cassie had all the powers of morphing available. Surely, if she were alive and OK, she would morph and fly home.

We spread out, far and wide, looking for any clue. And I guess Marco had finally found it.

Now, with all of us gathered together, Marco told everything he knew. He told how Cassie had revealed herself to the Controller, Karen. He told how she had saved Karen from the leopard with Marco's unwitting help. And he told how Cassie had allowed herself to be made into a Controller in a desperate ploy to save the human girl, Karen.

<She's an idiot!> Marco concluded savagely. <Right now that Yeerk in her head knows every-thing. Everything!>

<Why would Cassie do this?> Ax wondered. <It is obvious that this Controller must be eliminated.>

<Cassie must have had a reason,> Rachel said.

<Of course she had a reason,> I said.

<Yeah? What?> Marco demanded. <What reason could she have for giving us all up to the Yeerks?>

<You really don't know, Marco?> I asked him. <You really don't know why someone would not want to kill? Or even stand by and let someone else kill?>

<She has no choice!> Marco said.

<There's always a choice,> Tobias said. <I can't get mad at someone not wanting to take a life. I can't get mad at someone for thinking life is sacred. I just can't.>

It surprised me, him coming to Cassie's defence. Tobias lives as a pure predator. For him, killing is something he has to do for breakfast.

<This is a war,> Rachel said coldly. <We're fighting for our lives. We have a right to do whatever it takes to win.>

<Maybe we'll lose, maybe we'll win,> I said. <But if we win and someday it's all over, you'd better hope there are still plenty of Cassies in the world. You'd better hope that not everyone has decided it's OK to do whatever it takes to win.>

Everyone fell silent for a while, and we just flew hard. It was strange, the silence. I'm supposed to be the leader, although every day

121

that goes by I wish a little more that I wasn't. But one thing a leader does is try to understand his people. I understood them.

I understood Ax's near-silence. This was a matter between humans. Not his business.

I understood Rachel's anger. She felt like she was being accused of being immoral, compared with Cassie.

I understood Tobias, after thinking about it for a minute. Tobias is a human being living inside a hawk. Holding on to human ideas and human virtues is important to him. He values pity and kindness, because he lives in a world where there is no pity.

I understood Marco. Marco is one of those people who jumps right to the conclusion, without a lot of wondering and guessing. You could say he's smart. Or efficient. Or I guess you could say he's ruthless. He's not mean or cruel. He just gets from point A to point Z faster than most people.

<So what are we going to do when we get there?> Rachel asked after a while.

<I don't know,> I admitted. <Let's see if we find her first.>

<I've just found her,> Rachel said. <There's an osprey just breaking out of the trees. It's her.>

<I see it,> Tobias said.

We all saw it. And we knew that the osprey saw us.

Chapter 23

Jake

We flew towards the osprey, but it soon went below the trees and out of sight. It was quite a distance away, and we'd been in morph for a long time.

<We need to land and demorph,> I said.

<We can't! She'll get away!> Marco said.

<Ax? How's our time?>

<We must demorph, Prince Jake. Unless we wish to become trapped in these morphs.>

Down we went, spiralling down through warm updraughts, to land on the shady forest floor. We quickly demorphed, all but Tobias, of course. He stayed aloft, keeping an eye out.

Then, after a few minutes' rest, we morphed again and took to the air once more. Now we had a solid two hours.

But we had also given Cassie, or the Yeerk inside her, plenty of time to hide or escape.

We flew towards where we'd last seen her. Through the trees, we began to catch glimpses of a search force up ahead.

<Those are state police uniforms,> Tobias observed.

<We have to find Cassie and that girl Karen before they do,> I said. But I wasn't thinking anything more about it than that. We flew above the dozen or so cops.

Blam! Blam! Blam! Blam! Blam!

<What the. . .>

BamBamBamBamBamBamBamBamBam!

<They're shooting at us!>

Pistols, rifles, and even automatic weapons were firing up at us.

Flit! Flit! Flit!

The bullets whizzed past me, one so close the wind from it ruffled my feathers.

<They're Controllers!> Rachel yelled. <She warned them!>

<Just keep flying!> I said. <We'll be past them in a few—>

<Aaahhh!>

I looked left and saw Rachel fall from the sky. With peregrine eyes I could see the blood coming from her tail. She'd been hit! Hit too badly to keep flying. She'd have to demorph and remorph.

But the woods below were full of Controllers.

<Fine,> Marco said. <They want a fight, we'll give them a fight.>

<No,> I said. <It's what they want. Or at least it's what that Yeerk wants. Tobias! Keep flying, find Cassie! Everyone else, with me!>

Rachel dropped down towards the tree-tops. I could hear the human-Controllers yelling in savage glee.

I dropped like a rock. Nothing on Earth is faster in a dive than a peregrine falcon. I aimed straight for Rachel.

The air blew past me like I was in a hurricane. Faster, faster, the ground rushing up to hit me! Rachel was two metres from hitting the ground.

And just below her, a human-Controller waited, grinning, holding an automatic rifle.

Full speed! I raked my talons forward.

Shwoooooooop!

I hit Rachel hard. It could almost have killed her, except that I absorbed some of the shock into my legs. I grabbed and opened my wings, hoping to save some momentum.

"Hey!" the Controller yelped, sounding very human.

Now, let me put this in perspective. Rachel was in bald eagle morph. I was in falcon morph. They are both birds of prey. But they're similar, like a cocker spaniel is similar to a Great Dane.

The eagle was huge. The big white head

alone would have been too much for me to carry. The odds of me flying away holding her were zero. All I could do was hope to get her a few metres away from the Controller.

But even that wasn't happening. I took the limp weight of the eagle on my talons, spread my wings, flapped like mad, and fell like a rock.

"*Tseeeeeeeeeer!*"

From the sky there fell a grey and white missile. Ax flared his harrier wings, swooped neatly, and sank both talons into Rachel's bloody tail.

We were still falling, but now at least we were gliding away from the nearest Controller.

He stomped towards us. We hustled and dragged Rachel's unconscious body over sticks and rocks and through bushes. But the human-Controller was plenty fast enough to keep up.

<We have to fight!> I said. <Demorph, Ax!>

Ax released his grip on Rachel, fluttered a distance away behind some trees, and began to demorph.

The human-Controller saw me helpless with Rachel. <Hah-hah-hah! I have you now! Hah-hah-hah!>

What are you, the Joker? I thought.

Suddenly, something blew past, leaving trails of blood on the man's face.

"Aaarrgghh!" he cried and clutched at his eyes.

Marco sailed past. <They're coming!> he yelled. <It's fight or flee time.>

I looked to see Ax half-way into Andalite morph. Marco and I were still one hundred per cent bird. Rachel was out cold. Marco and I would have to pass through human morph before we could get into anything dangerous.

<Ax! Finish demorphing, grab Rachel, and run!> I said. <Marco, you and I are outta here!>

I could hear voices, even over the yelling and cursing of the injured Controller. Footsteps and large bodies shoving through bushes.

<Ax?> I said.

<I can carry her,> he answered.

Still not totally Andalite, Ax ran over, scooped up Rachel in his weak Andalite arms, and turned tail to run like a deer.

I flapped my wings, praying for a breeze, and skimmed across the ground. Marco was right behind me.

Four men appeared! We were flying straight at them.

They raised their guns, we flapped like lunatics and skimmed centimetres above their heads.

Blam! Blam! Blam! They began blazing away.

Flit! Flit! Flit! The bullets blew past us. But then we found that breeze, filled our sail-like wings, and rose up, up, up above the trees and out of sight.

127

Chapter 24

Jake

We met up a few minutes later, out of the paths of the human-Controllers. Ax easily outran the humans, even carrying the big eagle. It only became difficult when Rachel suddenly woke up.

<What are you doing? Put me down! I'm going back and to the guy who shot me and—>

<Rachel! Glad you're awake. Now, shut up and demorph!> I said.

I was frantic. The battle had cost us time. Too much time. And now Rachel demorphing and remorphing would cost us more time. <Marco, go after Tobias. See if you can help. Keep track of the Yeerk — what ever body it's in.>

<You have some kind of instructions for me, oh, fearless leader?>

<Yeah. I do. The Yeerk does not make contact with anyone. I don't care if it's in Cassie or that girl Karen. Neither of them gets away. No matter what.>

Marco hesitated for a moment. <You mean. . . ?>

<I mean, one way or the other, neither Cassie nor that girl gets away.>

Marco muttered a curse. <How did it come to this?> he wondered. But he flew away at top speed.

I felt sick inside. It was right that I make the decision. And it was probably the right decision to make. But oh, man, I felt like I'd swallowed broken glass.

<Hurry up!> I yelled at Rachel. I wanted someone to be mad at and she was the first person I saw.

Rachel quickly demorphed back to human. Because the eagle morph is merely DNA, when she remorphed it, the bullet wound was gone.

Ax decided to stay on the ground and I agreed. We were close enough that he could run. And we might need his blade. Rachel and I took off again.

I instantly spotted Tobias circling over a small meadow just a thousand metres or so away. We sped towards him. Marco was not in sight.

<Tobias! What's happening?> Rachel demanded.

<You really don't want to know,> Tobias said harshly.

We caught up to him and looked down at the scene below. There, a little girl, Karen, squatted in the grass, looking intently at a leaf.

I focused my falcon eyes and saw tears running down the little girl's face. Then, I saw what she was looking at. It was a caterpillar. It hung, squirming, from the bottom of the leaf.

I don't know how I knew. But somehow I did.

I landed a few metres away. Rachel landed beside me. Karen looked at us without surprise.

"It's too late," she said simply.

<What's too late?> Rachel demanded.

"She did it," Karen said. "She gave her life. I watched her for almost two hours. I kept expecting her to change her mind. But she did it. She gave her life for this little human girl. And because she thought she could make peace with one enemy at least."

Rachel and I stared in horror at the caterpillar. It was hanging straight down. It was shedding its outer skin, pushing the skin up its body. And even now it was carefully, cautiously, stepping out of its old skin.

"Right at the end, right before the two hours were up, I told her to stop. I told her she'd proven herself to me. I begged her to stop, to demorph." Karen raised her green eyes to me. "But I'd forgotten. I don't think the caterpillar could hear. At least not speech. She didn't know that I had seen enough. And now. . ."

<Cassie!> I screamed. <Cassie! Demorph! Demorph!>

"Too late," Karen said again, and slowly rose to her feet.

<Cassie!> Rachel cried. <Oh, God, no! Cassie!>

There was the sound of hooves and Ax arrived at a run. Karen looked at him and sneered. "Ah, of course, the Andalite *aristh*."

<What have you done, Yeerk?> Ax demanded. His tail twitched. <I'll destroy you for this!>

<NO!> Rachel yelled in a blinding rage. <NO! This Yeerk is mine!>

She began to demorph at top speed, flesh and face emerging from feathers and beak.

"You fools! Don't you see?" Karen cried. "She gave her life to make some small fragment of peace! We have a deal! Cassie and I made a deal!"

She looked from one of us to the other. I guess she found no pity or understanding in our weird, demorphing faces.

Karen turned and ran. She ran as fast as little girl legs could move on a swollen, bruised, and bloody ankle.

<Shall I get her?> Ax asked calmly.

"No," Rachel said. She was human for the moment. "Let her run. Let her feel what it's like to be helpless. I'll deal with her soon enough."

And with that, Rachel began to morph from human into the African elephant whose DNA was a part of her.

Karen staggered and ran and fell. She reached the edge of the meadow and crawled into the trees.

And that's when we saw the flash of black and brown. It fell, silent, from a tree branch.

It dropped straight down on Karen.

It opened its mighty jaws, bared its railroad spike teeth, and prepared to sink those fangs into her unprotected neck.

"Aaaaahhhhh!" Karen screamed.

I froze. I was in mid-demorph. Rachel was in mid-morph. Maybe Ax could save the girl from the leopard, but he wouldn't move unless I gave the order.

And I just froze. Did I think, *Good, let the leopard do our dirty work for us*? Maybe. I don't know if I thought anything very clearly.

"Oh! Oh! Oh!" Karen wailed as the leopard crouched over her, aiming for the perfect bite.

And then. . .

A hand! A huge, black, hairy hand came out from behind the tree.

Fingers the size of bratwursts closed on the

scruff of the leopard's neck. Huge arms flexed, massive shoulders lifted, and the leopard was suddenly hanging in mid-air.

<I don't think so, kitty,> Marco said.

He spun half-way around and flung the leopard about seven metres.

Chapter 25

Jake

We made a strange little group, there at the edge of the meadow. An Andalite. An elephant. A gorilla. A hawk. And me. I was human again.

In the middle of the circle we formed was Karen. Or Aftran, depending on how you wanted to look at it.

"What are you going to do with me, Jake?" she asked.

It shocked me, hearing my own name come from her. I mean, it shouldn't have surprised me, because I knew she'd been inside Cassie's head. But it made it all so terribly clear: nothing had changed. Our lives were still in this Controller's hands.

"I don't know what to do with you," I admitted.

<Sure you do,> Rachel said coldly. <Marco just saved her for me. Isn't that right, Marco?>

But Marco didn't answer. Instead he began to demorph back to human, shrinking within the gorilla.

Rachel moved her massive head and looked at Ax. <You're with me, aren't you?>

"Of course he is," Karen snapped. "Humans may be capable of wanting peace, but not the almighty Andalites. Go ahead, Andalite. You have that tail of yours. Go ahead, use it."

Ax looked at Rachel with his stalk eyes. He kept his main eyes on Karen. And he said, <I will do as Prince Jake says.>

I saw the shock in Karen's eyes as she looked back at me to learn her fate.

"You said you had a deal with Cassie. Tell me about it."

"If she would suffer the same fate that awaits me — a life without sight, without pleasure, without freedom — then I would do what she asked me to do," Karen said simply.

"And what did Cassie ask you to do?"

"To make what small peace I could," Karen said. "To let this host body go free. And never to take another human host."

"You'll do this?" I asked.

Karen nodded. "Yes."

<Yeah, that's real likely,> Rachel said derisively.

135

I took a deep breath. "Why will you do it? Why?"

Karen smiled a small smile. "We are not all like Visser Three," she said. "Some of us are just little Yeerks, unimportant nobodies who are caught in this war. Some of us also want peace. Some of us want to find a better way. But how can we give up everything and leave the universe to. . ." She jerked her head towards Ax. "To them? They'll never feel anything but hatred and contempt for us. Cassie . . . Cassie did not hate."

<Jake, stop listening to her! She wants to destroy us. She'll say anything she has to!> Rachel cried. <She'll tell any lie she has to! You can't let her walk away. She can't be trusted.>

<Cassie trusted her,> Tobias said quietly.

<This is insane! Ridiculous!> Rachel yelled.

She was right. What Cassie had done was insane. But it wasn't wrong. And I just kept thinking, as idealistic and naive and even dumb as Cassie's actions might have seemed, did I want to undo them all now? Did I want to destroy the meaning of her sacrifice?

Cassie had given her life, making an absurd, hopeful bet on peace. If I gave one order . . . her bet would be wasted. If I gave the other order, we might all die.

"I guess sometimes you have to choose between smart, sane, ruthlessness, and totally stupid, insane hope," I said, not even realizing I was speaking out loud. "You can't just pick one and stick with it, either. Each time it comes up, you have to try and make your best decision. Most of the time, I guess I have to go with being smart and sane. But I don't want to live in a world where people don't try the stupid, crazy, hopeful thing sometimes."

I looked at Rachel, towering above us all. "Rachel, I'm not going to give any orders. Each of us has to decide for ourselves right now."

I looked at Karen again and then turned away. I walked back to the caterpillar. I plucked up the stalk of the plant, and carried it carefully away into the forest.

Tobias joined me a few minutes later. And then Ax. And Marco.

Rachel didn't come, not at first.

But after a while there she was, human again.

We looked at her, wondering.

"Cassie was my best friend," she said, gritting her teeth to control the tears. "I'm not going to be the one to call her a fool."

Rachel reached out her hands to take the stiffening, drying chrysalis.

"I'll carry her," she said. "I'll keep her safe."

Chapter 26

Cassie

For a long time, I was gone.

Unconscious.

Unaware.

A worm in hibernation. The limited caterpillar mind not even functioning at its very limited level.

It was like I was dead, only there were still these faint, far-off dreams. Wisps of dreams, really. Nothing to hold on to.

Faint images of people and places. My parents, most of all. Not that I knew what those vague faces meant.

I was changing, but I didn't know that I was changing. I didn't even know that I existed.

I was inside a hardened shell. Hanging from the bottom of a leaf. I was becoming one of the miracles of nature. I was living through nature's own morphing.

Slowly, so slowly, I became aware. I stirred and shifted and my own movement woke me up.

My dried, stiff sack of skin began to crack open like an egg. It split, and I felt a new, strange sensation. The first new thing I had felt for a long time.

Air!

Now things seemed to be happening very quickly. I was pushing, squirming, trying to get out. Impatient.

I pushed and suddenly. . .

I could see!

In an explosion of awareness, I knew who I was. I was Cassie! And I could see again!

Colours! Like some lunatic artist run nuts, spraying everything in brilliant, iridescent, glowing, insane colours!

Compound eyes, I told myself. Then I laughed, because I still knew the term. I was back. I was me again.

But not the human me.

Compound eyes. And now, antennae that unfolded from the stickiness of the chrysalis and smelled all the delicious smells of the world.

I pushed further, harder. And little by little, I emerged from the chrysalis.

Then, at last, I unfolded my wings. They

were limp and damp at first, but I held them out to dry and harden.

They were made up of millions of tiny scales, almost like the skin of a reptile. But these scales glittered with colour.

It was funny, I suppose, because I was seeing colour the way a butterfly does, which is very different from human sight. To my fractured, compound eyes, I seemed to be a dazzling ultra-violet and red. But human eyes would see me quite differently.

Where my mouth should have been, there was a long, coiled proboscis. My life's work would be to flit from one beautiful, glowing flower to the next. To uncoil my proboscis and drink nectar from the heart of the flower. And, as if by accident, carry grains of pollen to the next flower.

I had been a caterpillar. Now I was a butterfly. I had eyes. I had wings. I would not live out my life as a slug.

Had I cheated Aftran the Yeerk? Had Karen known about caterpillars and butterflies? Maybe not. In which case Aftran would not have known, either.

I could almost have been happy. But now, awake again, alert, aware, all my human memories came rushing back.

How long had I been this way? What awful agony would my parents have endured? And my friends, did they even know?

I tested my wings. Sunlight had dried them.

I was what I was. A butterfly. I would live a short life in a world of flowers.

I wanted to cry, but my butterfly instincts told me I had work to do. Flowers, loaded with pollen, waited for me to help them live.

Chapter 27

Jake

I was sitting in science class, listening to some hopelessly complicated lecture about fungus when I saw the familiar flash of brown and tan shoot past the window.

<Jake! Jake! She's coming out!> Tobias said.

"I thought it was supposed to take at least ten days!" I said. The teacher stared at me. So did most of the class, those that were awake.

"Sorry," I said. "I . . . um . . . I'm not feeling too well. Permission to go to the nurse?"

"Wait till the end of class."

"But I have to be sick!" I cried, and ran for the door. No one argues when you say you have to be sick. They just get out of your way.

Seconds later, Rachel got sick, too. She also had to run. Then Marco left the classroom he was in. Marco, being Marco, told his teacher he had to rush out to put on one of those Nicoderm patches. "I'm trying to break the smoking habit!" he yelled. "Don't stop me!"

Twenty minutes later, we were all assembled around the little flower garden behind Cassie's house. That's where we'd moved the chrysalis. It had been hanging from its transplanted plant, amid the flowers, with Tobias staying near by, day and night, to protect it from predators.

Cassie's parents didn't know, of course. Three days had gone by. They were still hopeful that she'd be found. I didn't know what to tell them. Or when. Or whether I should just let them go on hoping.

We gathered around the chrysalis, which was split wide open. The butterfly emerged, little by little. Then, at last, it spread its beautiful wings.

"It was supposed to take a couple of weeks," I said.

<Cassie always was the fastest morpher,> Tobias pointed out.

Rachel was crying, which is a disturbing sight because Rachel doesn't cry. I guess I was, too.

"She's a butterfly," Rachel said. "She made it. At least now she'll. . ."

She broke down. It was nice that Cassie was a butterfly instead of a caterpillar. But it wasn't anything to celebrate. Not to us. Not to her parents.

Ax arrived in human morph, trotting a little erratically on his two legs. He bent over and looked closely at the butterfly, just testing its wings. "What is that?"

"It's Cassie," I said. "Emerging from the chrysalis."

Ax looked puzzled. "But this is not at all the body she had."

"No, that's what happens," Marco explained. "The caterpillar becomes the butterfly."

Suddenly, the butterfly simply took off. It fluttered away, off across the flowers, like it was shopping for just the right one.

"Naturally-occurring morphing?" Ax asked quizzically. "You didn't tell me."

"I guess it is natural morphing," I said. "And I guess it's better to live your life as a butterfly than as a caterpillar."

"Would Cassie prefer being this creature to being human again?" Ax asked. "Creee-cher. Cuh-ree-ture."

Rachel sighed. "No, Ax, of course not. We're just saying that this is better than her only other choice. Better to be a butterfly than a caterpillar."

"Ah. I see," Ax said. "But maybe she would like to demorph now."

"I'm sure she would," Marco said grimly.

"Then she should," Ax said.

Slowly, one by one, we all turned our eyes to

stare at him. Rachel did a little more. She jumped up, grabbed him by the collar and said, "Are you jerking my chain, or do you have something to say?"

Ax seemed a little surprised, to put it mildly. But he said, "Oh, I see. You didn't realize. Zuh. Re-uh-liiii-zuh. A very complicated word, 'realize'. And the 'z' sound makes my human mouth-parts tickle."

"Ax! Are you saying Cassie can morph?!" I demanded.

"I believe so," he said. "This naturally-occurring morph should reset the morphing clock. She has two hours to demorph."

"GET! THAT! BUTTERFLY!" I yelled.

Chapter 28

Cassie

I had to lie to my parents. I stuck to the truth as much as I could. I mean, I told them about falling in the river. I just left out Karen. And I told them I'd survived for three days eating mushrooms.

I was on the news. And in the newspaper. The headline was "Girl Survives Ordeal Eating Mushrooms".

I thought that was kind of funny. Like the ordeal was mushrooms.

I was interviewed a lot. And I was hugged a lot. For a couple of days my parents wouldn't let go of me. Which was fine with me.

But finally, at last, my life started to get back to normal. Normal, except for the fact that each day I woke up wondering: would this be the day the Yeerks would take me? Would this be the day my friends and I would be made into Controllers?

But days went by and there were no sudden attacks. At school, Chapman, the assistant principal and a major Controller, ignored me like he always did. Jake's brother, Tom, just made some crack about me and mushrooms, but that was it.

No attack.

And then, my dad came home, snapping his fingers and giggling. He lifted me up and twirled me around into a really bad dance. Probably the Frug or the Twist or whatever.

"We're saved!" he said.

"Ooookay," I said.

"No, we got funding! We got funding! The Wildlife Rehabilitation Clinic is open for business again, and back better than ever."

"No way!" I screamed.

"Yeah. It was weird. Suddenly this guy from UniBank calls up and says his daughter had heard about the clinic. He says she's been bugging him to contribute enough money to keep us open. The man actually said, 'So, tell me what you need so my little girl will be happy'. So I did. And he's sending the cheque over."

He laughed. "A good week, huh?" Then he hugged me like he'd been doing every eight

147

minutes since I'd come back. "Wonder who that little girl is? We owe her big."

I knew the little girl's name, of course. Karen. Karen, who had been made into a Controller to keep tabs on her father, the president of UniBank.

But I, too, wondered *who* she was. All I knew for sure was that she had not given us up to her fellow Yeerks.

Another week went by before I was sure. I was in the mall — with Rachel, of course. Since being a butterfly, I'd become more interested in colours. Rachel decided this meant I should have all new clothes. So she was dragging me from store to store, attempting to get me to understand the concept of accessorizing.

And that's when I saw her, standing off by herself, just a little distance from the woman who must have been her mother.

I went over to her, leaving Rachel in the midst of some sweaters.

"Hi, Karen," I said.

"Hi, Cassie," she said.

"How are you?"

She looked at me with those familiar green eyes and said, "I'm free, Cassie. She kept her promise. I'm free."

I couldn't say anything. Words wouldn't come out. I just knelt down and gave the little girl a hug.

One small victory. One girl free. One connection made with one of our enemies.

A very small peace.

"She would be glad you escaped," Karen said. "She tried to stop you at the very end."

I nodded, wordless still.

Her mother came and got her then. Karen disappeared, a little girl carrying a huge secret, her mind filled with things no little kid should know.

Kind of like me, I realized. Kind of like all the Animorphs.

Was I still an Animorph?

Yes.

It meant I would have to fight sometimes. But being an Animorph might also let me find other small victories for peace. Amid all the conflict and fear and rage, I could still look for the enemy who might become a friend.

It wasn't a perfect answer, but it was the best I could do.

"So?" Rachel demanded, holding up two sweaters. "Which one do you like? The green or the red?"

I thought of Aftran, the enemy. I thought of her swimming blind in the Yeerk pool, with only her memories of a brighter world. She'd told me that humans live in paradise. She'd turned her back on paradise to make a small peace.

"Both, Rachel. And I like the blue. And the

yellow. And that gross colour there. And the stripes. We live in paradise, Rachel, and we don't even know it. And we don't know when it might end. We'd have to be fools not to enjoy it while we can. So, whip out your credit card, girl, we're adding some colour!"

We moved David from my house to Jake's house. We didn't have any idea what to do with him long-term. He couldn't go home. He couldn't go anywhere. He was a hunted person. And we could not allow him to be caught. Not with what he knew.

The day after he witnessed his father as a Controller, we assembled in the woods. Cassie's dad was working in the barn. Even though it was still chilly outside and the sky was filled with clouds, we were tramping along, clutching our sweatshirts and jackets closed with one hand.

With the other hand we were carrying a large, divided wire cage. We'd passed poles through, front to back, one on each side. Cassie, Jake, Rachel and I each had a pole-end. David walked alongside, a little off by himself. Tobias and Ax were in the woods.

In the cages were two big birds of prey: a merlin and a golden eagle. The merlin was about a quarter of the size of the eagle. The eagle was one big bird. And heavy. My carrying arm was straining.

Both birds had been patients of Cassie and her dad. Both were going to be released. . .

"David's here to acquire his first morph. The merlin."

"Which one's the merlin?" David asked.

"The smaller bird," Cassie said. "They're very fast, very agile," she added helpfully.

"Faster than the big one?" David asked.

<You don't want to be a golden eagle,> Tobias said. <They're jerks. They go after other birds. Not to mention anything from a rabbit to a small deer. And I'm not kidding about the deer. I saw a golden eagle take down a young doe. Sank those talons right into the back of her head, boom, she went down like she'd been shot.>

"I want to do the eagle," David said.

A moment's hesitation. "Any special reason?" Jake asked.

"Yeah. You tell me I have no home. No family. Now I'm supposed to be in the middle of some war with aliens. If I'm in a war, I want to kick butt."

Jake nodded. "It isn't always about sheer power. That golden eagle is as big as a bald eagle, and we have problems sometimes with Rachel being a bald eagle because of the size."

"That bird has a two-metre wingspan," Cassie pointed out.

David nodded and looked down at the leaves and grass underfoot. "Did Jake here tell you all what animals to morph? Or did you pick them yourselves?"

"I'm not telling you what animal to morph," Jake said calmly. But it was that calm voice Jake uses when he's actually starting to get mad.

"OK, then I'll morph the eagle," David insisted.

"Here's an idea," I said. "How about not being such a jerk? We saved you from the Yeerks. We've been doing this for awhile, all right? We know what we're talking about. And Jake is the leader of this little group, so how about if you show some respect?"

"Who are you, my father?" David sneered. "You don't tell me what to do. No one tells me what to do. As for saving me, hah! That's a joke. You wanted the blue box, and now you have it, and you know what I have? Nothing. That's what I have, nothing. So thanks."

"Look, kid—" Rachel began.

But Jake gave a little shake of his head and Rachel stopped talking and just fumed.

"You guys all think you're so tough and so cool," David said. "All these battles you've been in and all. But now, here I am, the new guy — as usual for me — and you don't like me."

"No one doesn't like you," Cassie said.

David turned his head to stare right at me. "*He* doesn't. I'm not an idiot, you know. I can tell what people think about me. My family moves every couple of years whenever my dad gets transferred. I'm always the new kid in school. So I've got good at telling what people think of me. And now, here I am in this different school. And I'm the new kid." He shrugged. "So, look, maybe you like me, maybe you don't like me. I don't care. I'm here. If you use the blue box on me I'm one of you. But I'm not going to get pushed around. And I'm not going to be all, 'Oh, thank you, wise and wonderful Animorphs, for letting me join'. If I'm in, I'm in all the way. If not . . . I guess I'll walk away and try to figure out what to do. On my own."

The funny thing was, I kind of liked David's little speech. I like people who push back when they get pushed. I liked the speech. I liked the attitude. I still didn't like David.

But Rachel laughed out loud. "Oh, he'll fit in fine. . ."